The Gingerbread Man

by

Kim Turner

Christmas Cookies

The Gingerbread Man

Cover Art by *Debbie Taylor*

The Wild Rose Press, Inc.
PO Box 708
Adams Basin, NY 14410-0708
Visit us at www.thewildrosepress.com

Publishing History
First Edition, 2021
Trade Paperback ISBN 978-1-5092-4013-5
Digital ISBN 978-1-5092-4014-2

Christmas Cookies
Published in the United States of America

Hannah turned to look at him, an easy smile crossing her lips. His breath held tight and without asking, he bent. He expected her to pull away though she didn't, and the impact of his lips to hers was tender. He rested his fingers along the curve of her neck, touching her hair. He eased her closer to him and her mouth parted, accepting more.

He stopped the kiss and took his hand away. "I'm sorry, I was caught up in us talking and you're so easy to speak with and...I..." He hadn't any words, nothing save the apology and what had he done? She'd taken the kiss, but maybe he should have waited.

"Please, don't apologize...Sully." The silence accompanied them longer than a breath of moments. "I'm not sorry in the least." She leaned against his knee with a giggle.

"My kissing you is humorous?" he asked, holding his own smile with his question.

"No, our kiss was very nice..." She lifted her brows and the silence encompassed them once more, but this time the profound comfort of loving again settled inside him.

Dedication

For my sister, Wendi—"Run, run, fast as you can.
You can't catch me, I'm the gingerbread man…"

Acknowledgments

Thanks to Judy Baty and Peggy Henderson for helping me learn a bit about the fine art of raising chickens. Thank you Lynne Cagle for reading when I needed some help and for offering suggestions!!!

~

Thanks again to Marcia Scott for all the last minute help and weekly chats about books and being friends!

Prologue

Harper Falls, Wyoming, November 1875

The howl of the wind sounded like a lone wolf calling into the silver winter night. John "Sully" Sullivan tied his horse, Sage, to a tree in the edge of the forest. A homestead sat in the distance, smoke from the chimney leaving a trail across the stillness of night. He took a moment to blow a bit of warmth into his gloved hands and waited out a long hiss of wind as snow flurries began.

The place belonged to a woman who was widowed some time back. Her lone cabin and small barn were several miles from his own. He'd made a point for some time to keep an eye on her and the children. A boy around ten or eleven and a small girl. It wasn't his place. But no one else in Harper Falls would be willing to come this far very often, when it came down to it.

He'd seen her up close once when he'd helped a few men move her husband's body to the graveyard in town. Most in Harper Falls were placed in the cemetery by the church, and he'd stood in the distance for the short service, holding his hat in his hand. The woman, Hannah Tate, had waited, unemotional, and then led both children to drop a handful of dirt over their father and husband's wooden box. He'd met Lucas Tate a few times and found the man honest and hardworking. But a bout of influenza had taken its toll on many in and around the territory that year.

He'd decided to make it his duty to look out for her without her knowing. He wasn't even sure why, except for the fact he lived closer than anyone else in town and it seemed the place stayed a bit neglected. So, as it was, he came by every few weeks during the early morning hours to help with a few odd chores so she might not take notice.

The front windows held a hint of light, a candle maybe, but all was quiet as he made his way closer. It would be dawn soon, so he could do what was needed before she or the children stirred. His boots crunched into the hard packed snow as droves of more began to fall across him. A blizzard was expected, and she was alone with two children in the middle of nowhere.

Leastwise, there was no dog to alarm her to his presence, and the livestock were inside the barn. He made his way around to the opposite side to lift an armload of frozen lumber. It wouldn't take him long to stack enough for a few days on the dry porch, making it an easy reach for her or the children. He eased up the two steps and placed the wood piece by piece in a neat pile along the walls of the home.

He returned to the barn and grabbed several of the larger logs. Maybe he did know why he helped when he didn't have to. Maybe if someone had helped Sarah, things might have been different. Her face lingered in his mind. The war now ten years past, though on any night in his dreams the cannons and gunfire sounded as loud as ever. Echoes of her sweet laughter still woke him from time to time. But Sarah was gone. Taken by a war that left her alone to bear a child and him hundreds of miles away.

Sometimes the ache in his chest was as visceral as the gunshot he'd survived all that time ago. It had taken months for his shoulder to heal, though he reckoned his heart never would.

That was how he'd found himself in Harper Falls, out west trapping for a living. The small town had not been welcoming at first to an ex-confederate soldier. So, he kept his distance from most and traded his hides and pelts for all he needed.

He ambled back down the steps but as he turned, he caught sight of the little girl standing in the window, looking at him. She wore a white night dress, her light hair in disarray around her sleepy face. This presented a slight problem, but with any luck she'd go back to sleep and forget. He held a gloved finger to his lips and in a flash, she disappeared, and he headed back the way he'd come.

He mounted up on Sage at the edge of the forest and glanced back once more before heading off to check his traps. Maybe one day he'd find the nerve to speak to Hannah Tate. Yeah, one of these days that was just what he was gonna do.

Chapter One

Harper Falls, Wyoming, December 1875

Heavy winds drifted across the house, stirring up orange embers in the hearth. Hannah Tate added another log to the fire and brushed her hands together with a shiver. Winter was here plain and simple, and Christmas was coming in less than a month. The blizzard blowing outside had hindered her trip to town.

She used a cloth to lift the lid to the black kettle of rabbit stew and stirred the contents that had been simmering since morning. The house smelled of the hearty broth as well as cornmeal muffins that were cooling on the side of the old black stove. If the blizzard continued, she'd be delayed further in returning the sewing to the mercantile. She relied on both the sewing and the selling of eggs to bring in much-needed income.

There was nothing much that could be done about the weather, an expected nuisance several times a year in Harper Falls.

She turned back to the table where she'd rolled out sugar cookie dough and called to her daughter. "Gertie, come along. We can cut out the gingerbread men now."

"Coming, Mama." Her four-year-old daughter skipped into the room, fair curls bouncing along her shoulders.

"Clean your hands and you can get started." She nodded to the cloth on the table and set the rolling pin aside, laying the flattened dough on a board close to her daughter's chair.

"Yes'm." Gertie took her time using the rag on each hand and climbed into her seat, resting on her knees. "I'm gonna eat them all gone when we're done."

Henry joined them, shutting the door to his room and taking a look out the front window at the thick fall of snow that made visibility difficult. "Sure a coming down like Hades now."

"Henry," Hannah scolded, though it seemed he pushed limits more of late, to see how much it took to get a reaction out of her.

"Yes'm." He plopped into his chair and watched as Gertie took the cookie mold and pressed it into the dough.

Hannah tossed the rag to him with a lift of her brows, and he took it up with a roll of his eyes, cleaning his hands.

"Guess we ain't gonna get to town in this. We'll have drifts so high Santa Claus won't be able to find us." He sulked though he snagged a small piece of loose dough and popped it into his mouth.

Gertie held the mold and frowned. "Santa is too gonna find us. Ain't he, Mama?"

Hannah glanced at each of them in turn. "Isn't, Gertie. Of course Santa will find his way to fill our stockings."

As it was, those stockings might hold a bit of candy along with a new knit hat and mittens she had made for each of them. Money was tight and anything extra had to wait. It seemed repairs piled up at times, the corral in need of new boards all around, but that would have to wait. At least she'd managed to move all the chickens and hatchlings inside the barn prior to the harsher weather.

"See, Mama said Santa Claus can too find us, Henry." Gertie made another press into the dough. pulling the gingerbread figure free as she scolded her brother. "Mama, did you make gingerbread men like this when you were a little girl?"

"We made them every December to last all through Christmas. Of course we had ginger spice to flavor the cookies. No ginger now, but very yummy anyways." She smiled as she thought of her mother and father back East in New Hampshire. A recent letter with a bit of money had arrived weeks back as well as the invitation to return home. Their constant request since…Lucas.

She sighed. Her choices were strained over what might be best, even two years later. Influenza had taken her husband and their lives would never be the same, no matter where they lived. But this was home, the home her children knew and the place they had loved their father. She'd taken in more sewing and along with selling eggs and ten-week-old hatchlings, she had survived. This was home.

"Well, if'n it ain't real gingerbread, then why not call them sugar men?" Despite his challenge, he took the mold to cut a cookie into shape.

"I suppose you'll have no issues joining Gertie and me in tasting once these have baked. And we are pretending they are gingerbread men, aren't we?" She smiled at her daughter and laid out another cookie for her son to decorate.

Gertie gave an exaggerated nod and continued her

efforts in adding dried fruits, nuts, and sugars to the flat brown dough men for decor.

"I suppose." He sprinkled the sugar cracklings over the top of the cookie.

She handed the small bowl of dried fruits to him. "Henry, did you stack the firewood on the front porch yesterday?"

She'd forgotten to ask about it the evening before, often having to remind him of his chores.

He lifted his gaze and dropped it again to the cookie. "I forgot, but I'll get it."

That was odd. She had intended to praise him for doing his chores without her asking. "Well, the wood was stacked against the porch." It wasn't the usual way he piled the wood either, which was most often a tossed pile in disarray. Instead it was in a rather neat pile.

"I was hurrying with the blizzard coming, plum forgot is all. Who did it then?" Henry studied her for a moment, then added fruit to the cookie. "I got the hatchlings all covered in the back of the barn. Need to check the water for them and the animals too."

She said nothing for a moment. "I'm...not sure, but you can check on the animals in a bit. I've some cooling water for them. Jasper and Jeddie were baying, hungry, if you could leave them oats and a bit more hay for Bessie."

He nodded and continued with the decorating.

"It was the gingerbread man." Gertie grabbed the small tray of nuts, pulling it in her direction. "In the snow last night, he stack-ted up all the wood."

Hannah frowned. Her daughter's imagination was always rather magical. "The gingerbread man?"

Henry added a fruit nose to the cookie he was

decorating and smirked at his little sister. "No gingerbread man could lift all that wood. It takes me five trips from the barn."

"He is real fer sure. I seen him a'fore too." Gertie pulled another cookie closer to her and added dried plum strips for clothing.

"Gertie, it's all right to believe stories and magical things we read, but I'm sure no gingerbread man stacked up the wood for us." Hannah put the next cookie she cut before Henry. Who would have done the chore? The nearest neighbors were miles from them.

"No, Mama he's real and works at night in the snow in a big brown coat and he's all covered in ice and fur." Gertie pouted but was distracted by decorating further, her expression changing to a smile.

"Ain't no dad burn gingerbread man out there, but there is the boogeyman, he's real sure enough." Henry narrowed his eyes and showed his teeth, snarling at her.

"There's no such a thing, Mama said." The little girl looked at her for assurance. "Right, Mama?"

"There's no boogeyman." Hannah began cutting more cookies, placing them before both children to finish off the dough.

"Well, there ain't no boogeyman or gingerbread man neither." He argued further, sliding a completed cookie to her.

"No, Henry, there *isn't*. But I suppose if the gingerbread man wanted to stack up our wood, it wouldn't be me who complained. Perhaps someone from town was by." Hannah glanced at the window, avoiding the thought that it might have been Patch Jackson.

The owner of the Harper Falls Trading Post &

Saloon had been by several times the last months, making her concerned at his continued persistence. More than once he'd been vocal about his interest in her since Lucas' passing, making her uncomfortable, to say the very least.

"No wonder she still believes in Santa, might as well believe in the boogeyman and gingerbread man too." Henry grabbed the tray of decorations and pulled them his direction once more.

"Henry!" Hannah warned. She'd told him more than enough times to keep his knowledge of Santa to himself.

"Henry Lucas Tate, there is too a real Santa Claus, and he ain't gonna bring you nothing but a big bag of coal," Gertie mocked, not accepting her brother's ideas. For all of her four years, she could be rather feisty.

He rolled his eyes ignoring her as he pressed a gumdrop to a gingerbread cookie to make a hat.

"Let's decorate the cookies. Leastwise the wood for a few days is there." Hannah placed the first tray of decorated cookies into the old iron stove to bake. Maybe once she fed them a bit of stew, they would both be in a better mood not to bicker. "And Henry, mind you don't get too far from the house or barn with what's blowing."

"Ma, you think I could use Pa's axe to get a Christmas tree closer to time?" Henry changed the subject though he didn't look at her.

She studied him, having not allowed him the use of Lucas' shotgun, but they would need a tree to trim. "I think so. Let this blizzard pass for a few days and if you don't go too far."

"Can I, Ma?" His blue eyes widened, and a smile

found him, something she hadn't seen in a long while.

"If you are careful, Henry. Not too big a tree and not too far up the mountain when you search." She wiped her hands on a cloth and stirred the stew once more.

"I'm almost thirteen, Pa said that was old enough to use the shotgun." He didn't look up from the cookie before him.

"Well, you're outgrowing your clothing faster than I can keep you in something that fits, but you're eleven, mind you." She corrected, set on the rule of not using a gun until he was older.

"You're nothin' but a dadburn little boy." Gertie added her two cents, patting on one of the cookies. She giggled, always quick with her tongue in adding to her brother's frustrations.

"I've brought home meat with my slingshot and cleaned it for that stew right there, like a man would do." Henry glared her way with a hint of satisfaction.

It was true, he had become quite skilled at hitting small game for their meals and for that she'd been thankful. Her own attempts with the shotgun had not been very successful at all.

"Gertie, that's enough." She handed each another cookie to decorate. "My goodness, when we are trapped inside you two can bicker."

"Well, leastwise it's not so long until I'm thirteen."

She sighed. He wasn't going to give up the argument.

Gertie dusted the sugar sprinkles from her hands. "And I am going to be five years old on March seventh and Mama is gonna bake a big pink cake for me. But right now, I'm making the gingerbread man who lives in the woods. He's the one who stack-ted the wood for sure when it was snowin' last night."

"Well, he must be a strong gingerbread man indeed." Hannah gave in to playing along.

"Yep, he's a brown coat like a fur and a hat the same. You's both a sleepin' so you didn't see him like me." The little girl didn't give up her story as she worked.

"I'm gonna check on things in the barn." Henry got up and shrugged on his coat and stepped into one boot at a time near the front door. He went to the hearth to grab the heavy bucket of water and made his way back to the door, adding his stocking cap and gloves.

"Don't take too long, it's awful cold and the stew will be ready in a short while," Hannah called to him as he escaped them both through the front door. A whip of wind stirred the embers in the hearth.

Lucas' death had been the hardest on him. Gertie had been too young to understand, but Henry had been almost nine and a boy needed his father. His interest in the shotgun was enough to fray her nerves. Weapons were dangerous, and as it was, she worried that he carried Lucas' large knife when he was out. She strayed to the window to watch him about his chores in and around the barn. The worry of who had stacked the wood still rode the edge of her thoughts.

She turned back to Gertie. "My, but who do you have there?"

Gertie licked her fingers. "It's the gingerbread man who stack-ted the wood, Mama. He smiles at me when he does his work."

She angled a glance at her daughter. The cookie was a mess of browns with sugar on his head and shoulders. It didn't look like a colorful Christmas cookie so much as a big brown man.

"Gertie, he smiles at you?" Something in her daughter's voice sounded sincere, not playful or from imagination.

"Yes'm, he tells me like this to be quiet cause it's dark time and you and Henry's a-sleepin'." The little girl held her index finger to her lips. "Got snow on his hat and his coat like this." She pointed to the cookie before her.

Hannah bent beside her daughter's chair. "Gertie, when did you see the gingerbread man?"

Gertie looked up at her with big blue eyes much like her father's. "Last night. He stack-ted up the wood Henry forgot. Is he gonna have to sit in his room on account he didn't do his chores?"

"No, because I think he still did his other chores, but have you seen the gingerbread man before he stacked the wood last night?" Hannah pressed, concerned, that several things around the homestead had been repaired with her assumption it was Henry's doing.

Gertie spread more sugar across the cookie. "Lots of times. He fixed the barn door too. And he feeded the mules apples one night."

"And he sees you in the window?" she asked, her thoughts racing at the idea her daughter might really be seeing someone in the night.

"Uh huh, and I watch him when I wake up cause I gotta go." Gertie giggled as she patted fruit pieces in place on the cookie. "See this is like him in his big brown coat and black boots."

"Well, that's a very well-dressed gingerbread man,

Gertie." Hannah touched her daughter's light hair and turned to check the cookies in the oven.

Perhaps Gertie *had* seen someone. It might be it was time to pay more attention during the night, when her daughter woke to use the small bowl in the corner of her room. She couldn't think of anyone save Patch Jackson who might bother to venture this far. She shivered as she walked back toward the window.

Chapter Two

With a growled curse, Sully pulled up a trap from the edge of the near frozen riverbed. The early afternoon light remained cold and gray as his heavy boots crunched across the depths of snow. He inspected the metal jaws already snapped closed and glanced around. This was the third one today. Someone had sprung the traps that belonged to him, and it wasn't an animal that had done it.

He moved paces upriver to thicker brush and reset the metal trap again. Two catches today, a muskrat and a small beaver. The meat from both were stored in a wrap inside his saddle bags and the hides scraped and rolled until he could cure them. He glanced around as a hiss of cold wind carried the faint sensation of being watched. Hell, if anyone was watching, it had to be ghosts from the war who followed him out here to this godforsaken wilderness. Sometimes the brutal winters didn't feel much different than they had felt during the war.

He trotted to the next trap and found the same, though a pile of bloody innards told the story. Whoever was springing his traps was doing so for food. He grabbed Sage by the reins and moved ahead, though the small pack mule, Sampson, protested with several brays.

"Aw, ain't far to town. Drop these pelts and you

can go back inside the barn to your oats." He urged the animals ahead to the small road that would take them to Harper Falls.

He made this jaunt to town every few weeks to sell the pelts he'd cured and to buy the dry goods he'd need to prepare more. He adjusted his hat as the town came into view, bustling with people. His boots sank in a slush of mud and ice, a sure sign the snows from the recent blizzard were melting.

He tugged the horse and mule behind him as he made his way toward the Harper Falls Trading Post & Saloon at the center of town. He tied Sage to the hitching post and moved to the hides and pelts across Sampson's packs, carrying them through the overhang to the table.

He laid the pelts out and glanced inside the saloon door where men lingered at the small bar. Others sat at the poker tables and still others entertained the women Patch Jackson employed.

"That's a pile there, Sully." Zeke Cramer ambled closer, thumbing through the hides, a hint of whiskey lingering. "How many ya got?"

Sully pulled the smaller furs off the unrolled pile. "Busy enough when I can keep someone from springing my traps. Seventeen small and six deer hides, four beavers…nice ones."

Zeke pulled his coat tighter. "Someone playing with your traps?"

He tugged the beaver pelts free and laid them out across the tables for the old man to inspect. "A couple sets were sprung…happening now and again."

"All kinds coming through town these days, can't trust a one of 'em it seems." Zeke pulled a pencil from behind his ear and figured on the small ledger from his pocket.

"Gonna need bags of salt, oil, and a sack of flour too, Zeke." He added as Zeke continued with his figures.

"Comes to about…" Zeke took a deep breath and let it out. "Afraid the market's down a bit on beaver…How's forty dollars sound?"

Sully had calculated closer to fifty dollars, but the market had been off the last few months. But if he knew anything about it, Patch Jackson was holding back prices he'd make in the resale market. "Zeke, you holding out on me or has Jackson changed it all up again?"

The old man glanced inside the store and back. "Sully, I can't do much better, you know that."

"He letting you eat, Zeke?" Sully pushed, though it wasn't like the old man could control his situation. It was how Patch Jackson kept Zeke at it, feeding his need for the drink to keep him working.

"He eats fine and makes a right good living as if it's any concern of yours, Sullivan." Patch Jackson stood in the doorway to the trading area, leaving the saloon behind. A mountain of a man, with his left eye covered in a black patch. An apparent injury inflicted in a bad set of cards from what the rumors told.

Sully narrowed a gaze on the man as he folded the paper money Zeke placed before him. "Dollar amounts on pelts keep dropping for the seller, but it seems the buyer still makes his. Some things never change."

Jackson came down the steps in a huff, the man wearing a heavy leather coat unlike one anyone in Harper Falls could afford. "You tossing accusations,

Sully, because I don't take to be called a cheat by you *Johnny Rebs* who roll through here now and again."

"War's ten years behind us, or haven't you noticed? I call things like I see 'em." He lifted the bag of salt Zeke laid down beside the flour and oil. "Thanks, Zeke."

He made his way to Sage and Sampson outside the canvas drapes, storing his goods on the pack animal.

Jackson followed, still talking. "What is it with all you leftovers from the war, always finding your way here anyway?"

"War's been over some time now, Jackson. Times change. But I suppose some people never do." He stuffed the oil tins into the pack with a glance back.

Jackson folded his arms. "Ya know they say you war drifters are a dying breed, you can always sell your pelts somewhere else, Sullivan."

He eyed the man who well knew the closest place for that to happen was hundreds of miles through rough terrain.

"Oh, well, that is a might far haul then, isn't it?" Jackson smirked. "Seems I'm all you trappers around here got."

He'd saved a few of the best hides and come spring he would travel for a better price, but for now he was at the man's mercy. He said nothing more as Jackson was lured back inside by one of the ladies.

Zeke walked over and held out a spool of roping. "Here ya go, forgot this here twine."

He took the rope and lopped it over the saddle horn on Sage at the same time he saw her. The woman from the homestead, Hannah Tate, walked along to the market with her children tagging along.

"Oh, I know that look there." Zeke glanced off in the distance and back to him with a knowing smile. "She's a beauty for sure, make a man stop and look more than once."

Sully dropped his gaze, focusing on his work.

"That there's Lucas Tate's widow. She's in town now and again at her shopping, but she's a hard one." The old man folded his arms and leaned closer. "Patch got his eyes on that one, but she ain't givin' into his charms it seems." The old man cackled and tugged his coat tighter in the chill.

"Can't say as I blame her there." He'd never seen eye to eye with the way Patch Jackson lorded over all in town. He didn't pay what pelts were worth and his whiskey prices were high enough to keep a poor man out of the saloon.

"You might do well to mind your fences there. Woman's bound to be lonely without a husband. Sooner or later they all get like that." Zeke glanced back to where the woman had gone inside the mercantile. "Seems a man might find himself needing a wife. Someone warm to hold come the night."

"Not lookin' for a wife." With that Sully took Sage by the reins and mounted up. He urged the horse and mule ahead, though his mind drifted back to Hannah Tate.

She was beautiful. It wasn't like he hadn't noticed that as he'd taken on to doing the chores at her place. Ah, he had no business thinking about a woman like Hannah Tate. Though ten years was a long time for a man to be alone without the comforts of a woman and now he was a damn fool.

Chapter Three

The chill of the recent snow suggested more to come, as Hannah walked with Gertie and Henry toward the Harper Falls Mercantile. The jaunt to town was not the best choice given the cold, but the children had been cooped up for so long with the recent blizzard. It was good for them all to be out of the house.

She had Gertie by the hand as they walked along. In the other she carried the basket of eggs to sell. Henry followed behind, carrying a crate of her latest sewing for the mercantile. They'd dropped off a batch of a dozen hatchlings at the Feed & Seed and that had gained her a few dollars in much needed cash.

"Come, Gertie." She urged, the little girl dawdling as she led the way.

"Mama, the gingerbread man." Gertie slowed further, looking behind them.

She glanced across town where shop keepers worked, and people moved about their way. The streets were full of those idling back to town with the break in the weather.

"See Mama, it's him." The little girl pointed at a man mounting his horse, a pack mule tied off to the same animal.

"Yes, indeed." Hannah tugged her along. "Come, Gertie…it's too cold to dawdle, sweetie." For all the patience she tried to display for her daughter, the winds were downright freezing, and none of them needed to catch a chill.

Gertie stopped full in her tracks. "But Mama, it's him, the gingerbread man, the one that stack-ted all the wood like I told you."

Hannah turned once more, but Gertie's pointed finger dropped. "He's gone...now."

"Come on, Gertie, ain't no gingerbread man gonna be out in the cold like this anyway." Henry's patience wore as thin as her own. "I got a penny, how about some gumdrops?"

Gertie let go of her hand and trotted to follow her brother into the mercantile, the gingerbread man forgotten. Hannah sighed with relief as she followed them inside, closing the door behind her.

"Morning, Hannah," Naomi Hunter greeted as she folded a bolt of fabric and placed it back on the shelves.

Hannah walked closer, admiring the beautiful pink linen with red stitching. "My, this is beautiful."

Naomi agreed with a nod. "And would make a lovely dress for yourself or Gertie. This came all the way from New York City, and they originally got it from France. Quite expensive."

Hannah glanced at her daughter, who was occupied watching Henry scoop gumdrops from a jar on the counter across the room. She turned back to Naomi, a slender woman with light hair piled on top of her head and big blue eyes. "Well, it would be very nice, but with Christmas coming soon, I've other items to spend for I'm afraid."

Naomi turned as her own children ran down the stairs and straight to the candy jars alongside Henry and Gertie. "Now you girls get away from that candy. I mean it, Callie and Katie, right now. Cammie, grab A.J. She's no business climbing to those jars of candy."

She rolled her eyes. "Not like a one of 'em ever listens. But the weather's kept 'em cooped up and all. It's so good people are out and about again."

Hannah had to agree. "Yes, it was good for me and the children to be out today in spite of the cold, though I think the mules would have been happier to stay in the barn." It had taken some doing for Henry to hitch up Jasper and Jeddie, the stubborn animals reluctant to leave the warmth of the barn, given the winds.

"More's a-coming they are saying, not done with Old Man Winter yet, though I do hope it holds off until after Christmas." Naomi laid the bolt of material back in place on the shelf. "I worried as I hadn't seen you and the children for a while, and y'all being so far from town."

"Thank you. We've been fine, although running low on sugar and flour." Hannah handed over a small list. "And, when the children are free of the candy, perhaps you could add two of the large peppermint sticks to my bag, wrapped, please."

"I'll get those for you along with the other items." Naomi made off with the crate of sewing and returned. "And this is in time. I have two more crates to send home with you that I'll need back in two weeks if you can manage it. Seems a few new families in town from back East, and everybody needs some mending."

Hannah touched the pink fabric once more. "Yes, of course, I'll make sure to be on time with Christmas around the corner. The extra money will come in handy."

It had been a bit since she'd made Gertie a fancy

church dress, but there wasn't money to pay for the extras right now. She touched the cheaper bolts of fabric. Those would have to do. She could afford a couple of yards for a new shirt for Henry and a smock for Gertie to add to their surprises for Christmas. If she managed her time, the extra pay would pay for more.

"Is so a gingerbread man. I seen him right out that door there a-riding his horse," Gertie shouted to Henry and the Hunter girls, who had gathered around her.

"There's no such thing, you must be pretending. Gingerbread men aren't real," Cammie argued with Gertie.

"Am not pretending. He's a real man that helps at night sometimes and I seen him, even made a cookie looks like him." Gertie folded her arms. She was several years younger than the twins and their eldest sister, Cammie, who held baby A.J.

"Gertie, you mustn't raise your voice inside, nor argue." Hannah warned, then glanced to where Henry was on the other side of the store. He ran his hand down the smooth wood of a fancy shotgun in the window of the mercantile.

The single glimpse of her son was so much like Lucas, she held her sights on him for a long moment. He'd grown so in the last year, he was going to be tall…like his father had been. Once again, her heart died inside for what her children would miss by not knowing him for longer. He'd been a good man, a loving husband and father, and every chance she got she did try to remind them of that.

Two years had flown by. It seemed as if she'd been living in a tunnel that never let the light inside. While she didn't care for the likes of guns, it wouldn't be long before Henry was thirteen. He was set on what his father had told him about the shotgun becoming his own.

She turned to the counter as her friend returned. "Naomi, could I add two yards from this?" She showed her the bolt of cheaper fabric that had hints of green thread through a lighter mint color.

"Of course, this is a lovely color and good material too, thicker weave." The woman went about the task, yelling at her girls once more. "You girls go on to your'n chores now...I mean it. No more candy. And Cammie, take the baby up to her crib and change her for me, please."

"Yes'm." Cammie carried the baby and grabbed one of the twins to follow, the other following along.

Gertie returned to her. "Mama, Henry won't share the candy. I want to hold the sack."

He laid down a single penny. "Ain't paid for it yet, silly."

"Thank you, sir." Naomi pocketed the penny with a smile at Henry and continued with the task of cutting the section of material for her.

Gertie jumped up and down for the sack of candy, that Henry held higher. He crammed a gumdrop into his mouth and let her have the remainder of the bag. For all the times he picked at Gertie, there were times he was very good to her.

Henry eyed the yards of material Naomi was wrapping and glanced at her. She read the disappointment in his gaze. He wasn't getting a shot gun this Christmas and nothing more than candy and clothing.

"Thank you, Naomi. I'll have the sewing back first

of next week." She pushed the basket of eggs closer to her friend. "Three dozen, the browns are double yolks."

"Well, the price for eggs is up a little these last few weeks. Four cents each with six cents for the double yolks." She leaned to whisper as it wasn't wise to gossip with others around. "Though it seems every time we make a bit of profit, that Patch Jackson has a reason to charge us more for things at the trading post."

Hannah met the woman's gaze. The mention of Patch Jackson unnerving any time he was mentioned.

"Let's see, that comes to a dollar and sixty-eight cents plus your pay for the sewing and…" The woman figured in her head. "Minus the fabric, that's equal to eight dollars and forty-six cents I owe you."

"Thank you, Naomi." Hannah folded the money with the few dollars she'd gained for the hatchlings and placed them inside the bag over her shoulder.

Naomi nodded to another customer as Hannah led the children back outside. She held the crate of sewing but handed the empty egg basket to Henry. He took it and walked on ahead as she and Gertie followed.

"Oh, Mama, look at her." Gertie stopped to admire the small fancy doll in the window of the mercantile. "She looks like a real girl for sure."

Hannah took a deep breath. "Yes, but Gertie, she's very expensive. And you already have Clara, the beautiful doll Grandma sent to you."

The little girl beamed with pride, hanging onto the windowsill. "But Clara is sad and needs a friend. And this dolly would be a good friend for her to play with all the time. I can ask Santa to bring her."

"Let's go." Henry called back to them both as he reached the wagon, tossing in the egg basket.

Hannah tugged Gertie along. Her chest was heavy at the idea her children wouldn't have something they wanted for Christmas, neither this year nor the last. She laid the sewing items in the back of the wagon and helped Gertie inside the canvas covers out of the wind. "Wrap in the covers, Gertie."

"All right, Mama." Her daughter bounced toward the front of the wagon and sat on the pile of blankets there, pulling one over herself.

Henry shuffled up to the buckboard as she hesitated. "Henry, stay here with your sister. I won't be long."

"Yes'm." He glanced at Gertie in the back and then to her again, lifting his brows.

"I forgot I need a bit of thread what with all that sewing," she explained, though her son scrutinized her for the moment.

She made her way back inside the mercantile, glancing at the doll Gertie had admired as Naomi joined her again.

"Change of heart?" The clerk and her friend asked.

"I suppose I didn't want to spend more, but Gertie has admired the smallest doll there ever since you've had it in the window." She went on. "Yes, on a change of heart, but money is always tight it seems."

"She's two dollars." Naomi held the doll out to show her. "Real china face, hands, and feet, swirled hair, and crinolines underneath her dress."

"I'll still have to wait for now, but..." She glanced to the opposite window where the shiny new shotgun leaned in its holder. "And...how much is the shotgun there?"

"My, but you've sure had a quick change in your

ideas." Naomi led her to the weapon on display. "This is five dollars and twenty cents; course George won't allow any credit on the guns at all."

"No, I wouldn't ask for credit, but wanted to know the price of each. I'd like to buy several yards of that beautiful red material after all. I might could make a nice dress. One that will sell to make purchase of the other items closer to Christmas." If she could make a fancy dress to sell and manage to finish the extra sewing in the crates, she could purchase what the children would so love to have.

"That's a grand idea, with the new families in town, some of them rather wealthy from what I could tell." Naomi pulled out the bolt of material once more. "And some red thread?"

"Yes, and pink as well. Let's see." She touched several rolls of satin ribbon and lifted a dark pink. "And this. Thank you, Naomi, I'll be back with the sewing as soon as possible."

"See you soon, Hannah." Naomi headed to the back of the store to her work.

Hannah turned to leave once more. There was a bit of money saved besides her earnings, but as it was, she needed to hold onto all. Stepping outside the door and onto the mercantile porch, she went down the two steps and turned to go toward the waiting wagon.

Patch Jackson stopped her in her tracks. "Good afternoon, Hannah."

She held his gaze. "Good afternoon, Mr. Jackson."

He moved to block her path once more. His one good eye glanced the full length of her. The other was covered with a black patch, though she'd never asked what had happened.

"I do hope you and your family did well with the storm. It's good you made it to town today." He glanced behind them to her waiting wagon.

"We are quite well, good day, sir." Hannah answered, but he still held in front of her. She met his gaze with a hard glare. More than once he'd forced her conversation such as this and while he was handsome, there was nothing about him she would ever desire. He was not a good man. Evil, in fact.

"Come now, what's your hurry, Hannah." He placed the hat back on his head. "You know, I'd be happy to help you on your homestead should you have anything that's difficult for a woman. I could drop by as I have some time and see how I can help."

"I assure you that my children and I are fine on our own, and your continued persistence is not needed." She lowered her voice to a whisper, her pulse racing as once again she tried to pass him.

"I'm offering to help you. I have the means to make a real easy life for a woman like yourself..." He stepped even closer, and touched her arm. "You'd want for little...your children wouldn't go without."

Hannah sucked in a frantic breath. "You are out of line, sir." With that she shoved past him, not looking back. He gave a nasty chuckle but didn't follow.

"Henry, you take the reins." She pulled herself up to the buckboard, thankful her son hadn't seen the exchange.

"What's wrong, Ma?" Henry asked as he took up the reins and let off the brake, urging the mules ahead.

"Oh, no mint thread, but Naomi says the stage is due Tuesday," she lied, easing her hands together and fighting the urge to look behind them to see if Mr.

Jackson was still there. It wasn't the first time he'd spoken to her of his abilities to provide for her and her children, but he'd never put his hands on her until now. She forced her breath to steady, focusing on the snow-covered road ahead.

It occurred to her the man Gertie had seen was Mr. Jackson. The very thought made her sick to her stomach. Well, she'd be paying attention and get to the bottom of that. She didn't want or need the man visiting her homestead for any reason.

Chapter Four

The afternoon sun did little to warm the temperatures. Sully sat idle in a thicket of pine firs where he'd been waiting for hours. Someone was springing his traps, and he was about to get to the bottom of it. No one much made their way to this higher part of the river and given the cold, he'd a mind to head back to his cabin. But the trap near the riverbed held the remains of a small muskrat that was already dead. Frozen.

He took a deep breath and let it out, frost holding before his face. He rubbed his gloved hands together as he stood. He'd been waiting too long, and it was damn freezing. He'd have to try again another day. But a crunch of snow at the creek's edge alerted him, and he crouched again. Movement came from out of the trees on the other side of the trap.

Hannah Tate's son made his way along the edge of the water. He bent and tossed a rock into the falls, then tossed a couple of bigger rocks to break the ice.

Sully waited. And sure enough, the boy slowed near the trap and then sat on the bank, using his foot to pry the muskrat loose. He pulled the carcass free, and the snap of the trap echoed around him.

So, he'd found the culprit. He'd seen him numbers of times near the woman's homestead but never at night like the little girl who played at the window. Well, he'd expected to find the thief to be someone Patch Jackson had put up to the job. Now what to do?

The kid stood holding up the frozen kill, inspecting it closer. Well, now was as good a time as any, before he thought to skin the hide.

"Hey there!" He walked out of the brush toward the river.

The youngster glanced up and his mouth fell open. Startling him wasn't the best idea as the kid took off running. Sully chased after him, ice crunching under his boots as he tried to head him off. He closed the gap, winded but certain to catch up as long as the youngster held onto his catch which was slowing him down. He jumped a log and held the pursuit as the kid glanced behind him. He slid through a patch of ice and scrambled back up.

Sully slipped a knee to the ground in the same spot but was back up running in an instant. He wasn't going to hurt the kid, but he would have words with him and turn him over to his mother. He supposed he was being a boy, but he needed to learn this lesson. Playing with another man's traps wasn't something to do and he'd end up shot dead.

He topped the ridge as the kid slid his way to the bottom and raced toward the homestead in the distance. He jumped to catch up about the time the youth sprang up and Sully grabbed him by the coat, sending him to the ground with a thud. The muskrat corpse plopped to the ground beside him.

The boy tried to break free, flailing like a fish on a line. "Let me go."

"Most don't take very kind to their traps being robbed." He struggled to pin the boy between his knees.

The kid put up a strong fight, but soon gave up, chest heaving from exertion.

"You gonna kill me, mister?" The wide blue eyes held fear, like a cornered animal.

"No, but taking someone's catch will get you shot if you aren't careful." He fought to catch his breath, still winded from the chase. What the hell did he do now?

"If I let you go, you've got to promise me you won't run." He eased up, but the kid struggled again. "Nope, stop it. Ain't gonna hurt ya. Gonna talk is all." He loosened his grip. The boy scooted to sit up, eyeing him with suspicion.

"What's your name?" he asked, leaning back on his haunches.

But the boy jerked a knife from his boot and held up the blade, defending himself. The sun caught the edge of the hard metal, and Sully froze for a second.

"Hey, boy, I was doing right by you." He held his hands high.

"Well, ain't gonna let you kill me neither." The lad waved the weapon again.

He grabbed the kid's wrist and slammed him to the ground, pounding his hand until the knife fell. Sully lifted it and then got off the boy, relieved if nothing else that neither of them had fallen victim to the blade.

"You pull a knife, boy, you'd best be ready to use it. Look, I know you live at that homestead." He softened his voice in spite of the anger still coursing through him. "I wasn't gonna hurt you, but stealing from a man's traps and then pulling a weapon on someone...boy, you're heading for nothing but trouble. Now what's your name?"

"Henry. You gonna tell my ma?" the boy asked

and shoved his hat back to his head, staring at the knife. "That's my pa's knife, give it back."

"Nope, you're gonna tell your ma, and I'll give you the knife back when you earn it." He dusted his trousers of snow and nodded toward the homestead.

"Earn it?" the boy questioned.

He nodded. "Name's Sully. When you tell your ma about stealing from my traps and after you pay me back a few hides, you'll get it back."

The boy let out a sigh and added a nod. "All right. But it might be better if'n you did kill me. Leastwise, Ma ain't gonna be happy."

Sully gave a slight chuckle. He remembered well what it was like to take a licking from his pa, but his mother was all together a different story. Even a look from her was worse than the full whippin' from his father. "You don't think so?"

"Nope. She'll be real mad. If you let me go, won't do it no more and I'll get you some pelts." He tried to talk his way out of this whole incident.

"How long you been upsetting my traps? Seems a bit since I've made a catch and I think that's on account of you." He stood and the boy followed him up.

"Took the ones that froze is all. The smaller ones. Ma won't let me use the shotgun yet, not till I'm thirteen." Henry folded his arms. "Got my pa's knife to clean 'em and a sling shot."

"Sling shot?"

Henry pulled it from under his coat and held it out. "Made it myself."

"You ever get anything with it?" Sully admired the leather pouch and straps. "Takes some skill to get something with one of these."

He shook his head, stuffing it back into his pocket. "A squirrel once, but Ma made a real good stew of it."

"But that still doesn't answer the reason for stealin'." Sully waited, narrowing a closer gaze on the boy. "Or holding up a knife to me."

"No, sir." He glanced toward home and back.

Sully took a deep breath and let it out. "Tell ya what. You leave my traps be, and I'll fix you up with a couple of your own, teach you where to put 'em. Show you how to cure the hides you been leaving behind. You agree to it, and I'll give you the knife back."

"You'd do that, mister?" The boy's eyes brightened at the prospect. "You'd let me borrow traps?"

"Call me Sully, but first you're still gonna tell your ma." He winked.

"Guessing you're gonna go with me to make sure I tell her." Henry gave a hard glance.

"No sense putting it off." He winked and pointed to the muskrat. "Take him on, the meat's yours this time since you gotta tell."

The boy grabbed the animal and took a step toward home. "All right, but she ain't gonna like it a bit, I tell ya."

"Nope, well mas are like that, expecting the better out of us." He caught up to the boy who led the way with no hesitation.

"You live in that cabin on the bluff?" Henry pointed over his shoulder.

"You've been that far?" It was a few miles from the river and a bit of a hike from there.

"Sure, my pa said he met you." The boy slowed as they arrived at the homestead. "Just didn't remember your name."

"Yep, it's mine. Your pa and I talked a few times in passing," he answered, at the same time that Hannah Tate stepped to the porch, and he damn near forgot to breathe.

Chapter Five

Hannah stepped to the porch as Henry walked toward the homestead, followed by a man she didn't recognize. Her pulse raced at the sight of her son's face. He carried a dead muskrat and laid it beside the porch.

"Mama?" Gertie followed her outside.

She warned Gertie pointing to the house. "Gertie, inside this minute."

Her daughter did as told, shutting the door without another word.

"Ma'am." The man spoke and removed his hat as he and Henry stopped before the porch, both looking up at her.

She nodded and Henry glanced up, though he dropped his gaze again.

"Henry? What's happened?" Something was wrong, and her tone rose an octave, her pulse racing.

Her son looked up at her again. "This is Sully from the cabin on the bluff, and...and I...been taking the meat from some of his traps."

Her heart dropped inside her chest. "Henry, stealin'?"

The man nodded at her son. "I'm John Sullivan, ma'am. Most call me Sully. No real harm done."

"Thank you for bringing him home, Mr. Sullivan." Her breath caught at the depth of green in the man's eyes.

"Again, no real harm done, a boy's gonna do such from time to time." He shuffled his boots on the crunchy snow-covered ground.

"Henry, I thought you'd hunted the game you brought in?" she questioned him, not believing he would do such a thing.

"I suppose I lied. I just wanted to get supper like Pa and make you proud, but you won't let me use the gun. I'll get the strap, wait in the barn." Henry hung his head, not looking at her. Then he took off for a run toward the barn.

Hannah turned back to the gentleman. "Mr. Sullivan, I'm sorry. I had no idea he'd been taking from your traps. If you can tell me what I owe you, I will see that you are paid for the cost of your losses."

He juggled the hat in his hands. "Like I said, ma'am. No real harm done."

He was a handsome man, younger than Lucas, but she remembered her husband talking of meeting the man from the bluff. "He's a very good boy, Mr. Sullivan, but I will assure you of it not happening again."

"Ma'am, if I may." He stepped closer. "He didn't lie when I caught him. He fessed up to it. If it's fittin', he knew he had to tell you. Not an easy thing to tell a mama you done wrong. You might take it easy on that lickin' he's about to get. Like I said he's doing what a boy does till he learns."

Hannah glanced back at the barn and to him again. "I will handle my son, Mr. Sullivan."

"Yes, ma'am, I understand, but I've some extra traps. I know the game trail. I could teach him to trap on his own." He shrugged. "If you'd be approvin' of it.

Besides, I've his knife here, and he needs an opportunity to earn it back. I won't keep it."

"He took his knife to you?" Hannah held her fingertips to her lips and then folded her arms.

He nodded. "He was afraid, just protecting himself."

"Lands…" Hannah shook her head. She couldn't fathom Henry challenging with a knife. So many things with her son had become difficult, as if he were restless all the time. Much of it she'd blamed on the loss of Lucas, but a knife…

Gertie stood at the door her mouth wide in wonder. "The gingerbread man."

"Back inside, Gertie. Right now." She pointed at the door once more.

"You gonna lick Henry for stealing?" Gertie again.

"Gertie, now!" Hannah raised her voice.

She turned back to Mr. Sullivan. And in that moment, it dawned on her that he was the man Gertie had pointed out in town, the man taking care of chores on the homestead. "I appreciate your offer, but I suppose he has already caused you enough trouble."

He nodded, agreeing but glancing toward the barn. "Maybe take it easy on him like I said, and I'll teach him to catch his own meals, let him earn the knife back."

He turned, walking back the way he'd come.

"Mr. Sullivan?" She stepped to the edge of the porch as he turned. "My daughter seems to think she sees you at night, making repairs and stacking wood here on our homestead."

"Guilty as charged. Being neighborly when I pass this way." He shrugged with a lift of his brows.

37

"I can appreciate your efforts, Mr. Sullivan, but I can't pay for more than what Henry has taken." She sighed with relief it wasn't Patch Jackson she had to worry about, but what was she to think now?

"Ma'am, I'm not asking for money." He held her gaze for a long moment.

"I think it would be good for Henry to learn to trap, if he's careful, and I thank you for the work." It was a quick decision, but wouldn't it be the right thing for Henry to learn the correct way of things? And Mr. Sullivan had returned her son unharmed.

"I'll bring the traps by in a few days. Teach him to clean and prepare them first and how to stay safe working with the sets." With that he turned again and continued the walk from the homestead into the forest.

"See, Mama, he's the one who stack-ted the wood, like I said." Gertie was at the door yet again. "You gonna give Henry a lickin' like Pa used to do with the strap?"

Hannah pointed to the house again. "Back inside until I get back, Gertie, and stay away from the fire."

Gertie shut the door once more, leaving her to make the chilly walk to the barn. She'd never spanked either of her children, having left that to Lucas. How could she do this? And now she wished Lucas still here. Henry had never stolen or lied to her knowledge, but he had to understand those were offenses that were not acceptable. But to take a strap to her son...

She opened the barn door to hear Henry's sniffles. But he was standing there holding the strap his father had left in the barn for such a purpose. He held it out for her to take.

"Henry, why?" She held the leather, not wanting to

do this.

He shrugged not looking up. "Cause we needed the meat, and you won't let me use the gun. I thought maybe a few would be all right, but…"

"Stealing, Henry. What if Mr. Sullivan hadn't been kind enough to be so forgiving?" She wanted him to understand a lesser man might have gone far enough to take his life.

"Yes'm but I thought maybe if I took a couple no one would know." He turned and placed both hands on the wood of the stall. "Pa made me hold on here, an extra lick if'n I let go. I'm ready."

Hannah gulped, her pulse racing fast. "Well, how many licks did he give you?" And this very minute she sure hated Lucas for dying and leaving her.

Henry shrugged and glanced back at her. "Equal to my age, mostly."

"Eleven, then." Her voice cracked and she cleared it with a deep sigh. "Henry…"

"Pa used to say he had to do it cause if ya don't get your licks, you can't move ahead to put it behind you. That way we both forget about it and never mention it again, he'd say." Henry explained but he didn't look at her, still facing the stall.

Hannah swallowed back the tears. It seemed he was expecting punishment as a way to know it was over. Not that she understood having to do this.

She lifted the strap and took a deep breath and Henry braced. And with every ounce of energy, she yielded the strap and slapped it across her son's backside, outside his clothing. Henry stiffened but didn't move, only jumped with each contact the strap made. Hannah fought tears, her heart crushing inside her chest.

"I think that's sufficient." She sniffled, vowing never again. "Henry, I never want to do this again."

"Yes'm. I'll get to my chores now." Henry escaped then barn, though not before she'd seen his tears.

Hannah covered her mouth to keep her tears silent and sobbed, leaning against the stall. Never had she done something as uncomfortable, but Henry had expected it and…she burst into tears.

"Lucas…how could you leave me to this…how?" She placed her hands to her face and sobbed further, until Jasper lugged his large head over the stall and nudged her. She wiped her tears and gave the animal a good rubbing. "Silly mule, I'll get you boys fed."

Chapter Six

The afternoon held colder than most, ice hanging in the trees from another bit of snow the night before. Sully urged Sage to the top of the ridge. Down below, the Tate homestead came into view. A steady stream of smoke escaped the chimney, and the horse perked his ears. It had been a week since he'd returned Henry home to his mother, but today was to turn things around. He'd brought along traps he could spare so he could get the boy started on learning the safety around them.

He'd been surprised that Hannah Tate was allowing him to teach her son, but he suspected she was aware she needed the meat her son could gain for them. He slowed Sage and then urged the horse to a stop, the sky clear and bright even in the cold.

"Mama, the gingerbread man, the gingerbread man." The little girl stood on the porch, pointing. "See?"

He dismounted, giving the tot a smile. Little did he understand the name she called him, but she was a pretty little thing. He tied Sage to the porch railing as Hannah emerged, wiping her hands on a rag.

"Good afternoon, Mr. Sullivan," she called to him as he pulled Sage alongside her home.

"Ma'am, everyone calls me Sully." He tipped his hat, taken aback again by her beauty. Her skin was pale and her eyes large and wide, as blue as the summer sky. And as usual there was a strength in how she held herself, tall and proud.

She nodded with a hint of a smile. "Sully."

Henry bolted from the house, shrugging on his coat. "Hey Sully, you brought traps for me to use? Been waiting for you to come back."

He nodded at the boy's enthusiasm, untying a sack from Sage. "You gotta listen and learn how to keep yourself safe, like your Ma insists."

"Oh, sure…I will." Henry bounced off the porch and took the feed sack Sully handed off. It held a number of older traps in varying sizes. The boy struggled to get it across his shoulder and headed toward the barn.

Sully stepped closer. "I'll teach him to oil and clean the traps. We'll put out a few close by in a bit, maybe he'll get rabbits and such."

Hannah Tate nodded as she came to the edge of the porch. His mouth went dry on what to say to her. It was awkward to speak to a woman when it had been so long since he'd even had a real conversation with one.

"I do hope you'll be willing to join us for supper this evening, before your return home." She held his gaze. But then glanced behind her as her daughter came outside, hanging onto her coat.

"I…" He cleared his voice, uncertain of a meal with the family. "I wouldn't want to impose, ma'am."

"But you gotta eat with us, since you done fixed the barn door and stack-ted up the wood." The little girl spoke to him as her mother bent and buttoned up the coat.

"She has a point." Hannah stood again and of all

things smiled. "Since you won't let me pay you for your efforts."

"Yes, ma'am. I'd be obliged." He nodded and went toward the barn not looking back. Hell, he couldn't, his pulse racing in talking to her as he had.

He entered the barn, swinging the door shut behind him. Henry was at the table in the corner, the traps all laid out before him.

"Thank you, Sully, these are kind of rusted and old, though." Henry glanced at him with a smile, touching the most rusted of pieces.

"First lesson. Cleaning and understanding the parts of the trap so you know how they work. You get a rag and start oiling all the pieces on each, scrub away what rust you can, and they'll shine up a bit, you'll see."

"Yes sir." Henry went to work with the oil on a cloth.

"The animals may smell the rust and the oil, so scrub until all the oil is gone." He glanced around the barn and at the two mules and a lone cow in the corner. The barn smelled of the animals, chickens not withholding.

"How many chickens you got here?" He bent to peek in the small pens at the back of the barn.

"Got thirty hens and a rooster, they all lay good. Well, not the rooster." The boy grinned and continued his work. "We sell the eggs and raise a couple of dozen hatchlings at a time to sell in town."

"That's a lot of work with chickens and all." He inspected the inches-tall hatchings in a large tub.

"They smell up the barn, but Ma says come spring she's saved enough to build them a better coop, something to keep the foxes and other things out." The boy scrubbing hard on the metal he was holding.

He chuckled, and walked over to the mules. "Seen these two and the cow in your corral when I pass by."

"That yonder is Jeddie and the other Jasper. Cow's named Bessie, but we call her Bess." Henry went back to his work in oiling the smallest trap. "This one's smaller."

"For rabbits and squirrels." He walked back over after giving Jeddie a good pat. "I got a small pack mule too, Sampson, an ornery cuss."

"Jasper gets like that sometimes, don't like it none he has to plow." Henry poured more oil onto the rag and pressed to open the jaws of the smaller trap. "I can't say I much like it either, but Pa taught me and now Ma helps a bit."

"Hold up." Sully grabbed Henry's arm. "You like this hand?"

Henry nodded, eyes wide. "Course I do."

"Even this small trap can snap right through bones and leave you a one-armed man for life."

"I guess so, if'n I'm not careful." Henry stopped his efforts and drew his hand back.

"Open a trap with an iron like this." Sully pulled a metal stake from the sack and used it to pry the trap open. "Never clean it while it's set, but if you use this, it'll open far enough for a good cleaning. You won't have to pick your nose with your elbow one day."

Henry laughed, some part of that warming Sully's thoughts. It had been a long time since he'd talked to a woman, and now, he was laughing with the boy. And he was caught up for sure in Hannah and her children, like it or not.

"All it takes is one slip because your hands are near

frozen out there, or one second of not paying attention."
He nodded for the boy to go ahead with his work. "You
used your foot to help you spring that trap of mine. No
more of that either. You take this iron with you at all
times, or you return home to get it."

Henry nodded and put more effort into his oiling
the trap before him. "Think I might trap something
tonight?"

"Might. Games been good 'cept where a few of
mine got snagged." He glanced at the boy.

Henry didn't look at him. "Said I was sorry."

"That you did." He reached inside his coat and laid
down the boy's knife. He'd kept it long enough, and he
would need it if he was trapping.

Henry looked at the knife. "I know I owe you some
hides, gonna work hard to make sure."

He changed the subject, moving two of the traps
further away. "Besides mine you ever worked traps?"

"No, Pa trapped some, let me go a few times." The
boy kept at his work.

"Well, I want you to think about a couple of things.
If you're a trapper, you have to have respect for the
animals you take. You never leave the traps set that you
don't check them." He waited until the boy looked at
him. "In the cold like this some of the smaller ones
freeze, but not before they feel the pain of these jaws."

Henry eyed the largest trap in his hands.

"It's your job to do right by an animal you trap.
You check every day and kill fast on those still alive.
It's a bit of mercy to do it fast. In the spring and
summer, check more often. Morning and evening." He
took his time making sure the boy understood the
important things.

"Ma won't let me shoot the shotgun alone, but when she's with me. Holds her ears." The boy laughed. "Doesn't care for guns and all, neither does Gertie. She screams."

"Well, womenfolk don't much like guns, but you got a knife. You wear a heavy glove, grab the animal by the ears, and cut its throat, hold it till it eases." He shrugged. "It's not pretty, but it's supper on the table. Once a month you keep this up on cleaning each trap, keep your meat from spoiling."

"Yes, sir, Sully." Henry smiled as he worked.

"You and your ma go to town much?" He asked, curious for the most part.

The boy nodded. "She does sewing for Mrs. Hunter at the mercantile and sells the eggs. We both sell the hatchlings…but I give my money except for a penny to Ma. I buy Gertie gumdrops or licorice." Henry held up a loose chain.

"Extra, in case one breaks. Looks like you're about done then. What would you do if you come up on a bear in your trap one day?" he asked, leaning against the table and folding is arms.

"Well…" Henry continued his work glancing at him. "How big a bear?"

He chuckled but went on to explain things he needed the boy to think about. "How big a bear? No matter. First never run from a bear, they like the chase. Back away quiet, walk away keeping an eye and when you are out of sight take off. Wolves are different, the pack may even try to follow you, run like hell then, climb a big tree, but they may wait you out. A big cat comes along, get out of there, they aren't afraid of anything much. Let them have your catch."

"Sully, you ever got a bear?" the boy asked and removed the bar, easing the trap together.

"Sure. Several. Hides sell well, but the bear grease even better. But you get help like I said." He took up the traps and put them back in the sack. "The other thing is you watch the weather, if you can't make it to your traps in a blizzard you shouldn't set them."

The boy followed him outside to Sage. He tied the bag to the back of the horse. "You go tell your ma we'll be back in 'bout two hours."

"She knows, you already told her." Henry answered, running a hand along the horse. "Gonna save and get me a good horse one day."

He shook his head and mounted up onto Sage. "Go on. You want to be a man to trap, then you respect your ma with where you are each day."

Henry shrugged and ran into the house, returning in a short time. "She says to remind you about suppin' with us when we get back."

He held out a hand, and the boy grabbed hold and mounted up behind him. "We'll head north along the river, put out about four of these traps, and you can check them early tomorrow. I'll meet you now and again mornings when I'm checking my own."

"That's good, I hunt there some, see the animals but ain't so good with the sling shot." Henry adjusted his hat and wrapped an arm around his middle.

"A sling's a hard one. Shot gun's easy enough." Sully added, "But you'll have to wait until your ma is willing you can have one, I suppose."

"Ma ain't gonna let me have my pa's shotgun until I'm thirteen." Henry let out a heavy sigh. "I'm plenty old enough now, being Pa's gone."

"What're you twelve now?" he asked, not sure, though the boy was tall and smart when it came down to it.

"Eleven, be twelve next August." Henry smiled with pride. "So it won't be too long."

"Well, see mamas nowhere much like guns, I suppose," he explained as his own mother had been the same. "I'm sorry about your pa. Lost my own pa when I was about your age. Nothing easy about that."

"No. Ain't easy a bit." The boy's voice softened.

"The creek's up ahead." He nodded as the horse took a small rise. "Best a little farther. Your ma shoot any?"

Henry laughed as Sage walked beside the small stream. "She can't hit the broad side of the barn, my pa used to say."

He joined in the laughter, and the two rode further up river for a time without talking. The air was crisp and cold, and ice and snow still lined the ground. More would come this time of year, but he'd at least get the boy started on trapping.

"Sully?" Henry leaned around to glance at him. "You fought in the war, some say."

Well, he might have expected it. "There's always talk in town, huh?"

Henry delayed a moment but nodded. "Some of the boys I know, but my pa said you were a soldier come west to work. Said you were a Confederate fighting for the south."

He nodded. "I was."

"Did you ever see much of the fighting?" the boy asked, his voice rising an octave with his interest.

"Not many who didn't see the fight," Sully

48

explained, though discussing the war…"Sometimes it's kill or be killed, best left in the past with the war over."

"My pa's brothers fought for the North. I didn't know 'em none, was a baby when we came out here." Henry peeked around at him again as if waiting on a reaction he didn't give. "We were from New Hampshire a'fore."

Sully pulled Sage to a stop. "Head over by the tree roots springing up there, and let's put out that smaller trap, good place for another muskrat or something smaller. War isn't good for either side. Took a bullet in my shoulder, almost died."

"A real gunshot…did it hurt?" Henry eyed him with lifted brows.

"Sure, hurt like the dickens, but worse was trying to let it heal after the doc got the bullet out. Took months," he explained, though his gut clenched any time he talked of the war, and if he didn't know better his shoulder began a mild ache.

The boy slid from behind him, and he dismounted after. He handed off one of the traps from the bag. Henry went over to the edge of the river and placed the trap, using the bar to set it and backing away.

"Now, biggest danger, when you're gonna cover it, hide it a bit…one slip and…"

The boy finished his sentence with a giggle. "I'll have to pick my nose with my elbow." But he was careful, placing brush around the set trap and backing away with ease.

"Good, let's walk for now." Sully led the way, tugging Sage along behind them.

"Sully, you had a family back East, too? Did you own slaves there?" Henry asked as they walked along.

Sully didn't answer right away, let them walk a few paces. "Had an uncle, left me a bit of land, but after the war wasn't much to go back home to. A small place south of Atlanta. We sharecropped with a number of slaves, but my uncle freed ours long before the war, thinking it best."

"Was ya married?" The boy trotted ahead of him. "This is a good spot."

Sully handed him the next trap out of the bag as he caught up. "Had a wife, but she died in childbirth before I came home. Like I said, no reason for me to return there."

Henry held his gaze and then placed the trap. "Sorry. I know how it feels and all, I mean. We lost my pa, he got real sick and the doctor couldn't help him none. I didn't believe it at first and ran off, but then I knew Ma would worry more and she'd need help with Gertie who was little then."

"It's all right, been a long time now." He sucked in a much-needed breath in thinking of Sarah once more. The boy's chatting helped a bit, and he supposed it was good for both of them. Henry took his time bending close and splaying branches and dried leaves over the trap.

"Ma still cries sometimes at night; thinks I don't hear, I guess." He glanced at the boy as they walked along. He supposed a woman had the right to cry over the loss of her husband and in raising her children alone. The last of his tears over Sarah had come a long time ago.

"Ma should have supper ready by the time we get back, sure starving with all that work," Henry mumbled as they mounted back up on Sage.

Sully nodded, his own belly grumbling. "You wake early, boy?"

"Most mornings a'fore six, unlessen I stay up too late," he explained.

"You check these traps soon as you are up, make it early so you get your own animals fed and stalls cleaned too. Keep your ma happy, and she won't mind you are out to your traps." He gave the bit of advice based on his memories of his own mother.

"Yes, sir." Henry went on. "She won't let me forget the chores. And Gertie either, harps like she's my ma too."

He gave a hearty laugh. "Well. Best you do as the ladies say, you'll long learn it's easier."

Henry held on tighter as the horse moved downhill toward the homestead. "I reckon you're right."

Sully pulled Sage to a halt and let the boy down once more. He was famished, but now to sit with a family at their meal? To eat and have conversation with her. With Hannah. It had been years since he'd had a meal at a table with a woman, and he could only imagine as much as he wanted this, it might be a bit uncomfortable. Like being dressed in a fine suit inside a church, that kind of uncomfortable. But then again he'd watched Hannah for a while now, and it was darn time he got to know her better.

Chapter Seven

Hannah placed the basket of hot biscuits on the table, wrapping them in a cloth to keep them warm. She glanced at the table where Gertie was placing the forks beside each plate and went to the window. In the distance, the sun was giving its last hints of gold to the cold sky. She expected Henry to return with Sully at any moment, and her pulse raced at the idea of him sharing their dinner. Lands, why was she so nervous?

She ran her hands through her hair and replaced the fallen strands back on top of her head. "Does the table look nice, Gertie?"

"Yes'm, Mama, we never get to use the pretty tablecloth. Is it a special 'casion?" The little girl took care to lay the forks just right.

"Well, it's nice to use with company, is all." She followed with a deep breath and another quick view around the house. As tidy as it gets with two children she supposed.

"We didn't use this one when Mrs. Hunter and Callie, Katie, and Cammie comed to eat with us when they showed us baby A. J. was awalkin'." Her daughter held true to never forgetting anything and questioning everything.

"That was because it was us two ladies and a lot of little girls eating cookies with sticky fingers, but not a full meal." She wouldn't have pulled out her finer things for such, given all the sweet snacks they'd shared.

Gertie tilted her head, angling a glance at her. "The gingerbread man is a special guest?"

"Gertie, his name is Sully…Mr. Sully, and he's been very nice as you discovered to help around the house, and so the right thing is to invite him for a nice meal is all. Being neighborly is a very kind thing to do." She moved the plate of fried chicken to the center of the table and added the small bowl of gravy and the side of boiled potatoes with string beans. And cooling on the top of the stove was a blackberry pie she'd made a short time ago with winter berries picked a few weeks back.

"Is he gonna work some more?" Gertie's blue eyes gazed at her. "Cause now he ain't gonna tell me to be quiet at night no more when I see him at the nighttime?"

"I suppose he will do a few things in the day when he has time to come by. But Gertie, you mustn't ask him some of your questions while we're eating. I'm sure he will let us know his plans in time." There was no telling what might come out of her daughter's mouth, and at this point she was having second thoughts about a meal with Sully and her children. Her pulse raced as did her mind. Had she been too forward? Would he think so? Lands, she should have waited for a time, but something about him felt comfortable.

Henry bolted through the door, giving her a second to straighten her skirt before Sully waited at the door behind him.

"Sully, please, come in…supper's ready, I hope you are both hungry." She stopped, having spit out the words in a flurry of nerves.

He removed his hat, ducking to step through the doorway. "Thank you, ma'am."

Henry ran to the sink pump to wash his hands. "Come on, Sully, we'll wash up. Ma cooks the best fried chicken you ever ate."

"Henry." Heat rushed to Hannah's cheeks even if it was true.

Hannah ambled closer as Sully shrugged out of his coat. She reached for his hat. "Let me hang these here for you."

He relinquished both and walked to the sink pump beside Henry, following with the same wash up and grabbing the drying cloth her son tossed to him. He dried and folded the cloth turning as she lifted the coffee pot.

"Coffee?"

"Yes, ma'am. Thank you." He waited near the table, tall and muscular, more so than she might have imagined without the heavy coat. His soft brown hair hung across his brow and touched his collar. His beard was close trimmed and his eyes the softest green she'd ever encountered.

"You can sit by me." Gertie patted the chair next to her, never shy it seemed as she gave her best smile.

"You may sit where you like," Hannah offered as Henry took his chair, leaving Sully the choice of hers or the one beside Gertie. After Lucas died, she'd changed the seating, where two chairs faced two instead of there being an empty head of the table where her husband had been. Perhaps that had been a good idea all along.

"All right then, how about right here." He eased into the chair beside Gertie and gave her a wink.

"Do you like fried chicken?" Her daughter began, folding her hands under her chin, eyeing Sully.

"As a matter of fact, I sure do, very much." He lifted his napkin to place it over his lap as Hannah set a cup of coffee before him.

She returned with her own cup of the hot brew, and he stood to ease her chair back.

"Thank you." She took her seat, tucking her skirt under her.

"Ma, Sully and me got the traps set, four of 'em, gonna have meat by tomorrow." Her son's enthusiasm caught her off guard, but she was glad for the break in silence.

"That's good then." Some part of her was uneasy about the traps, but he did seem so happy.

"He did a good job on deciding the location, a good potential for a catch." Sully sat once more and waited.

"That's good, the meat will be nice." She added her opinion without reminding him of Henry's previous theft.

"Henry, would you ask grace, please," she whispered and glanced at Sully who bowed his head to her surprise.

Henry gave a slight groan but bowed his head. "Lord, for this bounty we give thanks. Amen."

She opened her eyes again, and Sully was looking at her but dropped his gaze as quick as her own. She picked up the plate of chicken and handed it to him first, but instead of filling his plate, he held it and handed her the fork.

She speared a small piece and then took another to place on Gertie's plate. "Here ya go, Gertie."

Sully offered the plate to Henry, who grabbed two

pieces of chicken. When she glanced up again, Sully was still looking at her. His eyes were warm and inviting. Wouldn't all in town be scandalized if they knew this moment existed? It wasn't proper for her to have him in her home. She could hear her own mother's voice of warning and etiquette, but things were sometimes different out West and her period of mourning was over.

"Mr. Sully, are you the gingerbread man?" Gertie asked with a mouthful of potatoes.

"Gertie." Hannah scolded. "Eat your food first."

Sully coughed but grabbed his napkin and wiped his mouth. "Uh, well, I suppose I'm not, but...I do love gingerbread cookies."

"We maked some of them, but we done ate them all gone." Gertie shoved a spoonful of potatoes into her mouth. "And I maked one that looked like you when you work at the nighttime. You look like the gingerbread man in my storybook."

Hannah shook her head as he glanced at her, eyes wide in question. "Well, I suppose it was Gertie who discovered you've done a bit of the chores here for us. In the cold night with your heavy coat...you do appear as the cookies she decorated."

"You're the gingerbread man." Gertie giggled and pulled meat away from the chicken leg she was holding, chewing with her mouth open.

He gave a slight chuckle and looked at her daughter.

"That was supposed to be our secret, let me be neighborly to help a bit." He winked at Gertie.

Gertie shrugged as she used her hands to talk. "And you said to be quiet, but I told Mama and Henry you were outside sometimes, but they ain't ever believed me."

"She can't keep no secret." Henry chewed and swallowed. "Ma, I've got to go upriver early morning to check the traps, not good to leave the animals to suffer long. I'll get my morning chores early and take off."

"Henry…" Hannah pointed to her own cheek, and he wiped his mouth. "I do hope you'll be careful, of course I worry."

"His trail is pretty quiet." Sully added with a nod toward Henry. "Up early and back early, let your ma know where you are each day."

"It's gonna be Christmas soon, did you know that Mr. Sully?" Gertie turned in her chair resting on her knees.

He swallowed. "I sure did."

"And Santa's coming for sure to fill our stockings all up with goodies." Her daughter gulped from her tin mug leaving milk along her top lip.

Sully picked up the napkin beside her and swiped the mustache away. "That's always the fun part of Christmas then, but my favorite part is any kind of pie."

"Me too." Gertie's eyes widened. "We got a blackberry pie that I helped Mama to make today. And see, we even used-ed the fancy tablecloth for company."

"Gertie." Hannah's face flushed. "Eat your supper please."

Henry eyed the stove. "We got pie, Ma?"

Hannah got up and lifted the pie, grateful for her son's interest. "Blackberry, last of the winter berries I have on hand for now, leastwise until we can pick more."

She took up the knife and began sectioning the pie and then putting a piece to one plate at a time, serving Sully first.

"That sounds good, won't tell you it's been a couple of years since I've had pie, 'cept in town a time or two." Sully accepted the treat along with her son and Gertie. She waited as he took a bite.

"This is a nice meal, ma'am." He went on, "Henry showed me where he needs a bit of help mending the far corral fencing. I thought if you like I could get to that tonight, and it won't worry you with the weather and chance of the animals breaking through."

She couldn't expect him to do more than he already had, and then what of this meal together and his presence? "We do need the repair, but I don't expect you to do that."

"It's no trouble, you've some wood in the back of the barn that'll work fine," he added, taking another bite of the pie and then sipping from the hot mug of coffee.

Henry jumped up and led the way, working himself into his coat. "No, we got it, Ma, won't take no time at all I expect with Sully helping me."

"*Mister* Sully," Gertie corrected her brother who rolled his eyes.

"Tell ya what, if it's all right with your ma, both of you and your ma can call me Sully. I like that better anyway." He glanced at the children and then landed his gaze on her as he ate two more quick bites of the dessert.

"Since you ask it of us." She smiled, though her nerves still seemed on edge.

He stood and wiped his mouth and set his napkin aside, taking time to fold it. "It won't take but a bit to get it repaired. I thank you for the fine meal."

"I'll make you a plate to take with you once you and Henry are done," she offered, and he nodded as he grabbed his coat and hat and followed Henry outside.

Hannah took a deep breath and began to clear the table. It had gone well, and now he was working once more. She'd not accepted Patch Jackson's advances. He was such a frightening man to most in town. How could she find interest when his intentions toward her were not good ones? Yet something about Sully was comfortable, though she was acting like a schoolgirl once more.

"Gertie, when you're done, wash up, and I'll read you a story. It's close to time for bed." She cleaned the stove top, dusting the crumbs into her hand, and tossing them into the pail beside the stove.

"Aw, but Henry gets to stay outside." Gertie yawned, stretching her arms high.

"Henry is working, and you are yawning, go on." She helped Gertie down from the table and sent her on her way.

"But I'm not tired." Gertie skipped to the corner where her doll lay in a tiny wooden bed. "And neither is Clara sleepy, so we want to read *The Gingerbread Man* story again."

"Go on, we've a trip to town tomorrow to take back the sewing and eggs. You'll get to see the Hunter girls then." She pointed toward her room. "And we can read the story again, it's on your shelf."

"Can I look at the Christmas doll again? I know Santa will bring her if I ask in my prayers." Gertie went to her room, returning to get help stuffing her arms into her night dress.

Hannah assisted and then continued with the clean-up of supper. She covered the remainder of the pie and biscuits and then went about washing dishes. She made a small cloth of another piece of chicken, one of the biscuits and a wrapped piece of the pie for Sully.

She had suspected things to feel awkward with him, but beside a bit of nerves, he was easy to talk with. She'd never even allowed herself to think of the possibility of another man in her life, but here she was wondering of that now.

"Oh, listen to me. He may not even be doing anything other than being neighborly as he said." Scolding herself, she shook her head.

She finished with the kitchen and stepped into Gertie's small room and smiled. The little girl was fast asleep outside the covers and holding her copy of the fairy tale about *The Gingerbread Man*. She lifted the blankets and tucked her daughter's legs inside, pulling the covers high and blowing out the single lamp.

She walked to the front window again and glanced out toward the corral. Henry and Sully worked close beside one another, and a hint of their chatter found her. But it was good to see her son smile as well as Gertie and even herself. A warmth flowed through her as she looked on as Sully continued to work. He was a nice man, wasn't he? Though she couldn't assume his thoughts were the same as her own, and making assumptions might not be wise.

Chapter Eight

Sully sat on the porch, sipping water Hannah had brought out for him and Henry. The boy had long disappeared inside at her insistence it was late, and he was to go right to bed. She'd returned from inside carrying a sack of the prepared meal for Sully to take home.

"I suppose I am to thank you once more...Sully." Her voice softened as she wrapped a shawl around her, stepping to the porch.

He stood, not wishing to outstay his welcome. She handed the food to him, and her clear blue eyes held him for a long moment.

"Please, sit for a bit." She idled closer, glancing out to the corral as he settled back to the step and drank down the last of the water. He set the cup aside along with the food.

She took the stairs to stand in the yard, seeming to admire the patchwork he had helped her son repair on the corral. It wasn't the best, but it would work till spring or longer, keeping her animals where they needed to stay.

"We got the worst places taken care of." He wiped his brow with a sleeve. The night air was cold, but good, hard work brought on a sweat every time.

Darkness had long set in, the sun having faded over the hilltops to the west, a faint glimmer of light holding the edge of the sky. The bit of glow outlined her features he should damn well know weren't his to study, but he couldn't help himself.

"Henry's so happy about you teaching him to trap, and I am sure the repairs to the corral are fine. He's needed a reason to smile for a long time." She spoke, though she didn't face him.

He held the continued view of her against the stillness of the cold dark sky. "He's a good learner. Listens to what I tell him." He rested his elbows to his knees. The boy had been quick to pick up hints about the repairs and traps. He'd also done some of the corral repair himself and had done a good job of it.

She ambled closer, her arms folded. "Well, he's been a bit of a challenge since…since he lost his father. Of course, you know of that, of Lucas. You were there, weren't you, when we buried my husband."

He took a deep breath and let it out in a slow exhale. He hadn't known she'd even noticed him among the men that came to help with the burial of her husband. "Surprised you remember given your loss at the time."

She glanced along the sky and of all things sat on the stair below the one he occupied. The brush of her side added warmth against his knee, and he didn't move from her. That was what he'd noticed about her first, her ease in being who she was. Her lack of hesitation in talking to him now that the uncomfortable meal was behind them both. Perhaps the dinner hadn't been so painful, but it had been a long time since he'd faced a woman for real conversation. He'd be lying though, if his ideas of her were nothing. He'd thought about her any time he was near the homestead.

"I remember faces so vividly, but wasn't acquainted with everyone at the time," she whispered, drawing her shawl around her. "Makes me wonder of living out so far, where...I only know a few people in town."

He shrugged. "Times like that it's hard to know who is who anyways."

"Yes." She glanced down to where her shoulder rested against his knee. "I knew you were the one from the cabin on the ridge, but your name escaped me at the time. My husband spoke of your acquaintance."

He caught himself wanting to touch the tendrils of brown hair that hung in swirls around her ears and across her neck. The ones that had strayed from the pile on her head. He glanced away, not owning his own thoughts where she was concerned at this moment. Hell, it had been so long since...

"He said you fought for the south but had made a life here after the war." Her voice was soft and sure, not at all like his own uncertain nerves. "We were here before the war began. My husband didn't much believe in that fight, though his brothers did. He wanted us safe...and that was all. And now..."

"Not much left for me after the war ended. Came out here for work, like most." He glanced to her and back out into the night.

Seconds passed before she spoke again, but the quiet between them was something of a comfort.

"Tell me of her then." She glanced out across the homestead, studying the small barn.

His gut clenched tight enough to suck the wind from his lungs, and he shook his head. What had given him away? Talk in town? A man's life followed him no matter.

She turned to look at him, as if she read his thoughts. "A woman knows."

He supposed all he could do now was answer. "Sarah." It took a moment in speaking Sarah's name to compose himself, but he went on. "We lived south of Atlanta, but when the war started, I was sent north through Tennessee and Kentucky. I was gone months at a time, but close enough to be home twice."

The wind hissed around the eaves, and she shivered, giving him a moment more to gain his thoughts. Why was she so easy to talk to? How were his words even coming forth when he'd never much talked of Sarah before?

"I rode detail to get messages thru the lines but took a bullet outside Chattanooga toward the end of the war." Funny, when he spoke of it his shoulder gave a strong ache as it had earlier. He'd been decorated for saving the regiment from attack. After the bullet was removed, he'd suffered terrible fevers for months with the hopes of being well enough to travel home. But then news of Sarah had arrived…and what he knew of the world had come crumbling down right on top of him.

She kept her gaze on him, not pressing for his answers as he drew his words from depths where he'd hidden them away for so long.

"She was alone, and it was time for her to deliver. No doctors to be found south with the devastation of the war. A midwife tried to help but was too late for her or the baby girl." His pulse raced and he forced his breathing to slow. "I was recovering in a tented hospital south of Chattanooga. Never went back when the war ended. Couldn't." And he hadn't spoken to anyone at all though it would be those in town that would have the talk. Drifter. Confederate. Johnny Reb.

"It's good to speak of things," she said, her voice dropping lower in tone. "I think it helps the children that we remember and talk about their father often. I'm glad you told me, though I realize I asked. We share the same pain, Sully."

He nodded in agreement. "Maybe so."

"I'm sorry if I intruded, but...my mother always told me I had not been born with the will to hold my tongue." She laughed and something inside him warmed. "Much like Gertie, I'm afraid. Lands, she can and will say anything."

"Haven't talked...about Sarah for a long time, and I enjoyed Gertie's company at supper." And he had. The small girl was a happy little thing, full of questions.

Hannah turned to look at him, an easy smile crossing her lips. His breath held tight and without asking, he bent. He expected her to pull away though she didn't, and the impact of his lips to hers was tender. He rested his fingers along the curve of her neck, touching her hair. He eased her closer to him, and her mouth parted accepting more.

He stopped the kiss and took his hand away. "I'm sorry, I was caught up in us talking, and you're so easy to speak with and...I..." He hadn't any words, nothing save the apology and what had he done? She'd taken the kiss, but maybe he should have waited.

"Please, don't apologize...Sully." The silence accompanied them longer than a breath of moments. "I'm not sorry in the least." She leaned against his knee with a giggle.

"My kissing you is humorous?" he asked, holding

his own smile with his question.

"No, our kiss was very nice..." She lifted her brows, and the silence encompassed them once more, but this time the profound comfort of loving once more settled inside him.

Chapter Nine

Darkness held to the windows as Hannah added another log onto the fire at the hearth. The children had been asleep for a few hours, but as usual she peeked in on Gertie, who lay curled in her blankets. She pulled the cover higher on her daughter and touched her warm cheek. She eased the door to leave a bit open for the heat and turned the knob to Henry's room, peeking in at her son. He lay on his side, an arm hanging off the bed but snug in his blankets. She lifted his arm and put it underneath his covers and studied him for a long moment.

He'd grown so much in the last few years, so wanting to be a man but still so much a boy. And he'd be grown in no time at all, as fast as time moved, and for that she wanted to slow the days. He had worked hard alongside Sully, and she was proud of him for learning more about trapping.

She exited his room and sat to her sewing for the evening. She'd cut the patterns for Henry's shirt and had finished tacking the pattern together, adding the collar. She sat threading the needle, struggling in the light of the candle on the table. Drawing the thread through the mint garment, her mind wouldn't settle.

Sully had kissed her. She supposed neither of them had expected that to happen, but it had. He'd left a bit later, and she'd watched until he disappeared into the darkness of the hills. But a kiss, and her emotions were perplexed. If anything, she had welcomed his touch, sat close so maybe he would.

She hesitated with the sewing and touched her lips which still tingled. She had wanted the kiss, had even thought of it long before the meal they'd shared. Some part of her wanted to weep over Lucas, but he was gone and there was little that could be done. She'd had no right in asking Sully about his wife, but somehow, she had known he'd once been married. And now what of them? No promises had been made. A smile and a touch after the tender kiss. He hadn't even said goodbye other than to hold her gaze for a long moment, leaving her to wonder of his thoughts on the matter.

She wasn't sure what had come over her other than the need to feel close in that moment. To feel something again that was her own, to feel like a woman. Now she lingered with the want for more and her hopes that her choices were the right ones for herself and her children. She hadn't thought of marriage again, but now it crossed her mind. He was a good man, a kind man, and wasn't it all right to think of herself and the future of her children?

****

Sully scraped a beaver hide, the gray sky hinting at more weather, and the cold bitter. Sleep had evaded him, and he didn't have to think hard about the reasons.

Hannah.

He'd spent over a year watching her from the edge of the woods, careful not to be seen, uncertain why. But now, he'd kissed her and opened up feelings he wasn't sure he understood. Images of Sarah had crossed his mind all night, giving him a restless slumber.

Sometimes in his dreams he could almost touch her, though she'd always wisp away out of his reach. But last night she'd faded from view, leaving Hannah there in the wake of his dream.

He'd never expected to kiss her, at least not as he had after sharing a meal and a short time of knowing her. His love for Sarah had been that of a smitten young man in hopes of a long life together with his bride. But touching Hannah was altogether different, and he wasn't sure why.

The war had taken it all from him, his home, his land, a wife, and even a child he'd never known. At times the pain had been so great he was sure he'd die of it. But he hadn't, and finding Hannah had for the moment opened his eyes to the idea he might find what he'd lost once more. Maybe as it was if he played his cards right, didn't rush her, and let them learn each other, the idea of marriage and a family would be enticing. He'd been alone for so long now he wasn't sure of anything.

He stretched the hide across the board and tacked it into place. Then used his knife to trim thin portions of the hide, careful not to take more fur away. He tacked it one small nail at a time, letting his mind wander, hoping for distraction if nothing more.

Henry would be out at his traps this morning, and with any luck, the boy would have a few smaller animals. He'd been very receptive to learning. And even in repairing the corral fencing, the boy had listened and helped without any back talk or laziness. He was a hard worker. And the little girl thinking he was a gingerbread cookie man had made him laugh. Laughter. Something that had evaded him with living alone for so long.

He pulled to stretch the hide with the last tack and began with the salt, covering the white powder all across the hides to every edge. He sucked in a deep breath. He shouldn't have let the kiss happen. But he'd been powerless not to reach for Hannah. She'd tasted of warmth and of the spring in the harsh dead of winter, and all he could think about was touching her again.

He stood and inspected the hide. Good enough. About fourteen days, this one would be ready for trade along with about six others, though he was gonna have to fight for a price he deserved. That or travel to get a better payment than that bastard Jackson was handing out.

He peered into the graying sky and squeezed his gloved hands tight against the cold. He glanced across the treetops of his home on the ridge, high enough to give him a visual for miles. And somewhere south further than his view…well, there was Hannah. And now, he was lost to thoughts of her once more. Maybe he was, but he did need to check on Henry and start teaching the boy about curing hides. He grabbed a pouch of salt and headed for the barn to saddle Sage, letting a smile cross his face.

Chapter Ten

Hannah measured the dress she'd sewn for
Hunter's Mercantile. It was a gamble, but the pale pink
taffeta garment was beautiful, some of her best work. If
it would sell prior to Christmas, she might make enough
money to spare. She might afford the doll for Gertie
and maybe, much to her chagrin, the shotgun for Henry.

He hadn't asked, knowing he had to wait until he
was older, but with him out to his traps each morning,
she fathomed his having a gun might be the lesser of
evils. If he were careful and if Sully could teach him
how to care for it. As it was now, Sully had taught him
the simpler measures of curing the smaller hides he'd
gathered. The barn was laden with several drying hides
he'd be able to sell to make a bit of money for himself.
That was good too, wasn't it? Though she would have
to say between the animals, chickens, and the hides, the
barn did carry a rather staunch fragrance. It would be
nice to have the creatures and hides outside the barn
come spring. And she'd hopefully have the money to
allow Henry to build a bigger chicken coop.

Sully had been by several times, but neither of
them had mentioned again the kiss. She hadn't been
sure of what to say. Maybe the accidental kiss marked
them as friends who shared the same pain. They both
knew loss, and the tender moment would allow each of
them to move ahead of the place they'd found

themselves dwelling.

Still, she'd found herself lying alone in her bed at night with thoughts of getting to know Sully better and the possibility of marriage. And shameful or not, she'd thought about what it might be like to lie in her bed with Sully and allow his touch. Lands, her thoughts…

She wrote out the measurements to the dress and pinned the mark up to the front of it. From time to time, she had sold dresses and perhaps with Christmas not far off, someone would see fit to make the purchase. She hung it across the display board, thinking it was so pretty she should have kept it for herself.

Giggles from upstairs filtered to her, and she couldn't hold back her own smile. Gertie always loved the chance to play with the Hunter girls.

Naomi touched the sleeve of the dress. "Hannah, this is about the most beautiful dress I've ever seen. Fancier than anything I could order from back East. I am sure someone might come along who is interested."

"Well, here is hoping so." She admired the garment once more.

The giggles found them again and both ladies laughed. "My girls love for Gertie to play."

"She was so excited about coming to town today." Hannah brushed across the dress again as the bell on the door of the mercantile rang.

She turned, and her heart bolted to a stop. Sully removed his hat, making eye contact and giving a nod as he went past them to his shopping. They hadn't discussed anything of the possibility of seeing each other in town and now…

Naomi glanced at her and then moved toward him. "Mr. Sullivan, how can I help you today?"

He hesitated, and Hannah turned back to the dress, her heart racing.

"Need some penny tacks and cord, ma'am." He stepped with purpose toward the rolls of twine and cord as Hannah repacked her bag and set it aside. It didn't take long for Naomi to assist him and take his payment.

"Ladies." He tipped his hat and left the store.

Hannah turned back to her bag and the dress. Lands, just being near Sully again made her heart race and her thoughts fray.

Naomi drifted closer eyeing her with speculation. "Oh, Hannah?"

Hannah lifted her gaze to her friend as if she hadn't seen the exchange between her and Sully.

"Hannah, I seen how he's a lookin' at you. A man smitten sure enough," Naomi whispered with a smirk of sorts. "Do you know Mr. Sullivan?"

"He's helping Henry learn to set his traps and tan hides," she explained, hoping that would be enough not to give her away.

"He's a Confederate. Lost his wife in the war and showed up out here years back. A war hero some say, saved a whole regiment somewhere near Chattanooga and got himself shot. But was honored in spite of the south losing." Naomi continued to whisper. "Maybe it's a meant to be for you two lonely hearts to meet, Hannah. He is so handsome and much like you, alone."

Hannah shook her head, focusing on the dress once more. "Naomi, it's not like that."

"Maybe it should be. I worry of you so. Lands sakes, what would be so wrong with that? He's kinda quiet when he comes in but very polite any time he's here." Naomi leaned closer. "And maybe if'n you and he became acquainted so to speak, that Patch Jackson would mind his own business about you."

She moved the dress again to straighten it. "Naomi, he's helping Henry a bit is all, like I said."

"But he's a looking like he knows you, so you bake him a pie or something." The bell at the door rang again, and Hannah gave quick thanks her friend was back to her work once more. Naomi had her best interest in mind, and she did know about Mr. Jackson's advances toward her, but sharing about Sully, well, not now.

She walked to the stairs to call Gertie. "Gertie, it's time for us to leave."

"Aw, Mama," came her daughter's reply. "I'm playin' dollies."

"Come on. We'll be back with another batch of eggs in a few days." She coaxed, and a pouting Gertie made her way down the stairs.

She waved to Naomi and led her daughter toward the door, helping her into her coat and tying her stocking cap what with the cold winds. She called to Henry across the muddy snow-covered road. "Henry, we're ready."

He came trotting over, though he climbed up in the wagon, sitting on the buckboard with a huff.

She lifted Gertie up beside him. "Henry?"

"That Mr. Jackson is a cheat, like all in town say." He folded his arms, narrowing his brows.

"What's happened?" She asked, waiting for him to look at her.

"He gave me three dollars for the hides I had, said I was young, and he couldn't trust they'd been cured well." He showed her the money and shoved it back into his pocket with shake of his head.

"Sully said you should get about three to four dollars a hide." She'd heard him telling Henry as much. Patch Jackson was not a fair man and lorded over all in town where he could and now, he'd cheated her son.

He gave an angered shrug. "He said the market's down, that's all he could give me today and that ain't right."

Hannah glanced at the Trading Post where Zeke waited outside. "Henry, wait here, get Gertie inside the wagon into the blankets. I'll be back." She placed the sewing basket inside the back of the wagon and returned.

Henry's mouth fell open. "Ma, where ya going?"

"To have words with Mr. Jackson. Now you both stay here, and I mean it, watch your sister." Hannah scolded, then turned to march right toward the Trading Post & Saloon.

Her pulse raced, and while facing off with Patch Jackson wasn't her idea of an easy task, she was not going to let him cheat her son. She stepped inside the canvas where men and women traded items, which was full of men exchanging monies and pelts with Zeke.

She approached the old man who most often she'd found kind, but very much a man who did as his boss told him, right or wrong. "Mr. Cramer, might I ask what is the going price for pelts of small animals, rabbits, and such?"

Henry had tanned several small rabbit hides as well as one beaver, but he still deserved a fair price for his efforts. Six in all if she was remembering right.

"Well, we are able to give up to four dollars for the nicer ones, thick and tanned well. Sometimes three when the markets down a bit like it is now." Zeke placed the hat back to his bald head, the lingering smell of stale alcohol wafting around her.

"Where might I find Mr. Jackson?" She kept her voice tight and glanced toward the inside of the saloon.

Zeke shook his head. "Well, he's inside the saloon at the game, don't much like being disturbed, ma'am, when he's a playin' poker."

"I care little what he prefers." Hannah stepped past the old man and up the few stairs entering the saloon. She'd never been inside before, and smoke lingered in a heavy haze. She coughed. Several men turned to look at her and she spotted Mr. Jackson at a table in the corner with four other men, indeed playing poker.

She moved to the table around a saloon girl.

"Welcome, missy, but this here's my end of the saloon. Don't fancy the competition, if you'll get to your business and be on your way." The woman gave her a toothless cackle sizing her up with a glare.

Hannah ignored her and moved ahead, stopping before Mr. Jackson. "Mr. Jackson, I'd like a word please."

He glanced up at her with a lift of his brows. "Well, Mrs. Tate, I'm rather involved in an intense game at the moment as you can see."

He turned back to his game, discarding and taking another card from the dealer.

"Mr. Jackson."

He ignored her further.

Hannah took a deep breath, her nerves frayed. When he tossed his chips to the center of the table she slammed her hand flat on the middle, scattering the chips piled there. The saloon went silent.

"My son had three pelts, small, mind you, but well cared for, and I am here to collect his correct payment, sir." Hannah held herself steady in the dreaded quiet.

Jackson crushed out his cigar, blew out a stream of smoke and raised his head to look at her. "Was that your boy?"

"Indeed." She answered what he already knew.

"Well, his pelts weren't in the best of care." He chuckled and continued his game.

"I want my son's rightful money this instant; you've given him three and he is owed six more. If you prefer he does not trade here, we won't do so, but I will expect him paid as well as any." Hannah spoke, aware she was angering him with the narrowing of his gaze on her. "He was taught how to care for the pelts and has done a fine job of it."

"Honey, come with me. I like a woman with a bit of fight." One of the other men laughed.

She ignored him. "I'm waiting."

Patch Jackson chuckled but nonetheless reached into his coat pocket and tugged out the bills laying them before her. The cover over his one eye made it difficult to judge his level of anger, but she'd no doubt he was not happy with her. So be it.

She reached for the pile, but Jackson slapped his hand down onto hers. "Your boy said he learned to trap from that no-good Confederate, Sully."

Hannah held his hard gaze, fighting not to show her fear, though her pulse raced.

He grabbed her wrist, pulling her to his face. "You keeping company with the likes of Sully, are ya? I'll warn you to watch yourself then. Never know how things may go for a man like him."

She jerked her wrist away from his grip and took up the money, never dropping his hard gaze until she was outside the saloon. She'd done it, but challenging Patch Jackson wasn't to be taken without pause, and now she would worry for herself, her children, and...Sully.

Chapter Eleven

Sully waited upstream as Henry went about checking his traps. He'd come on foot to see for himself how the boy was doing with learning his way around the catch and tanning hides. The morning sun fluttered through the trees, leaving him to believe the afternoon might give a bit of warmth for a time. Henry bent to free the animal from the trap before him and lifted the small gray fox.

That would be a nice one, cleaned up, but the boy still needed a gun. Hannah had remained reluctant on the issue, afraid for her son, and he supposed he understood, but it wasn't his place to say anything more.

Henry laid out the fox and began cleaning the animal, but he stopped, glancing around him.

"Good instincts." Sully stepped ahead, though the boy startled for a moment and then continued his work. He walked closer and looked on as Henry did a fine job of gutting and skinning the animal.

"I knew someone was there. Felt it like you said. That how a bear might make me feel?" Henry used his knife with care, prepping the animal for saving as much of the hide as he could.

"Nope, you'll hear a noisy bear and the wolves, but a cat might stalk you a ways. That instinct will serve you well." He moved closer, the boy doing a fine job of things. "Who taught you to skin like that?"

"Pa did." Henry didn't look up. "On the smaller things like rabbits and squirrels. Be a might easier if Ma would let me use the gun come spring. Won't none much freeze to death like this when it warms. Gonna need a way to kill 'em easy like you said, with respect."

"I think ma's are like that sometimes, not liking guns and such." Sully glanced around them, his rifle across his shoulder, uneasy himself at this point. He, looked around as if someone was near. "I'll follow you back home, show you about tacking out this hide to look even nicer than the rest. This will bring you about six dollars if you do it right, let it dry well, and care for it."

"He's a beauty. Might think to keep this one for me. First one and all." Henry glanced up at him, the boy's blue eyes telling. "Mama had to make that Mr. Jackson give me a fair price on the other furs you helped me with."

Sully bent to a knee, concerned. "Patch cheated you?"

"Tried to, but Ma got the money I'z owed." Henry freed the hide and folded it in on itself. "But…she don't say much, he's sweet on her, and she don't like talking to him. I ain't supposed to hate, but I hate the likes of him. I think he scared her when she asked for the right money and all."

Hanna was a tough one, but Jackson was evil at best, the bastard lording over most in town. "He harasses your ma then?"

Henry angled a glance at him. "She ain't said nothing, but I seen him try couple of times to kiss her. I think he wasn't real nice to her when she went into the saloon. She was angry but didn't say much after."

"He ever harmed her before?" he asked, his pulse racing at Patch even taking a look at Hannah.

"Nahhh, don't think so." He placed the hide in his fur bag. "My pa didn't much like him neither, said he was crooked and cheated most in town. Sully, why do they let a man like that stay and run things then?"

"Jackson's a cheat to most. Tell you what, he does that again, doesn't pay you the right amount for your hides, let me know. Don't tell your ma, let's keep her from having to deal with him. Might be best if you stay away from him too." He would put a stop to Patch Jackson for cheating the boy again if that happened.

Henry glanced up with a nod. "All right. I can save up some more hides and then go when you're there. Does he cheat you any, Sully?"

"He tries." That was about the best answer he had for now. Patch Jackson cheated anyone he could. But the fact the man was harassing Hannah had him a bit unnerved. He'd be lying to himself if Hannah hadn't stayed on his mind day and night, but he hadn't thought of her having dealings with Jackson.

Henry stood, gathering the bag over his shoulder and adjusting his hat. He began the walk toward home, leaving Sully to his thoughts for most of the jaunt.

Smoke flowed in a steady dark stream from the cabin chimney as the house came into view. Covered in a spray of golden sun, the cabin still held snow and ice lingering in piles around it and the barn. He stole a glance behind them, still carrying the feeling of unrest, but no one was there.

"You got some tacking boards left since you've been working other hides?" he asked, adjusting the pack across his shoulder as he and Henry arrived at the barn.

Jasper and Jeddie moved to the edge of the corral fencing. Sully gave them both a pat and chuckled.

"I got a bigger one Pa had in the back; I'll get it." Henry took off inside the double doors of the barn and returned a short moment later, a large frame in both hands. "Pa used to use this one if the animal was bigger."

"I got you some salt when I was in town, got some extra for me too. You get started, and I'll take a look at the fencing again. See what we might repair a bit more before spring." He handed Henry the linen bag and laid his pack against the barn wall. He ambled toward the corral and checked on the work they had done.

The front door of the cabin opened, and Gertie hopped down each step, with Hannah close on her heels. Her gaze met his as she came closer to where Henry worked.

Gertie bounced along and eyed him as he returned to where Henry was scrubbing the wooden board off with a dust cloth.

"Watcha doing, Henry?" the little girl asked as she bent close to watch all her brother was up to. She was a cute little thing, with light curls and inquisitive blue eyes.

"Gotta clean this board to tack out the fox there," Henry explained with a nod to the hide he had unrolled and laid out beside the board.

Gertie wrinkled her nose for a moment but then turned to him. "Did you killed-ed the fox?"

"Henry got that one there on his own," Sully answered her as he lifted the pouch of salt and laid it within Henry's reach.

The boy went right to work in knowing how to cover the hide to draw out the moisture once he had it tacked down and stretched.

Gertie got up and began skipping around again, humming and then singing out loud. "That might be the fox that ate the gingerbread man all gone like in my book."

Sully glanced up when the little girl giggled, stopping before him. "What's so funny?"

"You're the gingerbread man." She laughed again and skipped all around him and her brother over and over, singing the song. "Run, run. Fast as you can, you can't catch me, I'm the gingerbread man."

Sully shook his head and growled out his words. "Maybe I am...and the gingerbread man tickles little people like you. You better run for sure."

She took off with a bloodcurdling scream and laughed so hard it didn't take much to catch her. He scooped her up and tickled her, putting her back to the ground, her cackles contagious.

Hannah joined them, her own laughter bringing him a smile.

"Get me again, Sully." Gertie ran on a giggle, and he chased her once more and grabbed her tossing her into the air and catching her. He chuckled along, it being a long time since he'd played with any little ones as such.

He placed her to her feet once more as he stopped before Hannah and smiled. "Afternoon."

She wore a light brown coat, but it was open given the lesser cold, with the near noon sun. Her blue blouse was tucked into a brown skirt, and she wore dark boots accenting her height, still a foot lesser than him. But she was a beauty, and he'd known that for a long time now, but from afar until Henry had gotten into his traps. Maybe as it was, he should thank the boy for that, one day.

"Good afternoon, Sully." Hannah approached, folding her arms.

"Come on, get me again, gingerbread man," Gertie yelled as she skipped near Henry, her arms swinging. "Run, run fast as you can, you can't catch me, I'm the gingerbread man."

Hannah laughed. "Gertie, let Mr. Sully help Henry."

Sully glanced at the little girl, and she squealed and skipped further away. "It's fine. Nice to hear a little one giggle and play. Henry, you doing all right there?"

"Yes, sir, got it covered, smoothing it out better." Henry continued with the salt, leaning over the hide to cover it. It was good to see the boy taking to his work.

"That's good work there, you keep smoothing and fill in all the gaps. I need to show your ma the inside stalls." He turned back to Hannah with a nod for her to follow.

"I know they are in need of repair as much as the outside corral you and Henry worked on." Hannah stepped in behind him, and he slowed to let her catch him.

"Nothing that can't be fixed, but your mules are chewing at the top rails." He opened the barn door and waited for her to pass through first, hints of flowers intoxicating his senses.

"Here." He moved to where Jeddie and Jasper stayed when inside and traced the top wood of the stall, dust flying. "They're chewing a bit, leastwise one of them."

Hannah nodded, glancing where he held the wood of the stall. "I suppose I've noticed but thought it might wait until summer. But I fear neither Henry nor I know much about how to best do things when needed."

"This will be an easy fix, but ornery mules are going to chew a new one too. Might put a little turpentine with a cloth along the wood and deter them a bit." He leaned over the corral to take a look on the inner side. "I'd double board it for a bit more protection."

She stepped closer to peer over the stall, so close to him he gulped for a breath and his thoughts frayed.

"Oh, I do see. But I suppose I might not have known it was so bad." She ran her hand across the boarding and then yelped jerking her hand away. "Splinter."

Instinct pushed him, and he took her hand and inspected, spotting the culprit. He touched too close, and she jumped.

"That's it. Ouch." Her gaze met his and in spite of knowing better, he lifted her palm toward his mouth.

"What are you..." She didn't finish.

Sully used his teeth to extract the fraction of wood. He spat it away, but didn't let go of her hand.

He drew her closer, and with an ease he hadn't expected took her lips. She leaned into him, and he delved deeper tasting, unable to stop himself. He'd been longing for this since his first taste of her.

"Won't apologize this time," he whispered, not intending to let her go.

"Then don't." she leaned into him, and he placed

his lips to hers, wanting far more. So, he gave her what they both sought, teasing and tasting, because he'd thought of nothing more since the last kiss. Damn, but it had been so long since he'd felt the softness of a woman, the tenderness of plump lips teasing him back, and the taste of sweetness.

"Mama?" Gertie pushed through the barn door, bouncing inside, eyes wide as she stopped before them.

Sully dropped his hands and turned back to the corral, busying himself with the chewed wooden areas. Well, of all the luck, but then again…children did such.

"Yes, Gertie." Hannah faced her daughter, turning from him.

Sully grabbed a twine of roped cord, gathering it up to tie it together.

Gertie looked from one to the other. "Mama, Henry won't let me help salt the fox skin."

"Well, Gertie, Henry has his way of doing things," she explained. "He's very proud of getting that fox and wishes to prepare it himself."

Sully walked across the barn and hung the coil of rope on the loop by the work bench, his pulse racing at having touched Hannah once more.

"But I wanna sprinkle salt on the fox too," the little girl whined, stepping closer.

"Gertie, go and play. You and I have the wash to do today, and you always help me with the folding." Hannah shuffled her daughter toward the barn doors.

Gertie turned to her and glanced at him. "Why did you kiss the gingerbread man, Mama?"

"Gertie, that's enough. I had a splinter in my finger, and Mr. Sully removed it is all." Hannah glanced back to him with a shake of her head scooting her daughter from the barn.

"I'm sorry, but not surprised. Gertie is observant about everything it seems." The blush across her cheeks enticing.

He chuckled but shrugged as she walked closer again. "It was bound to happen; guess I should be more gentlemanly."

She smiled. "Guilty as charged of kissing the gingerbread man."

He stepped to her again and took her into his arms, drawing her against him. "I wasn't quite finished."

"No?" She lifted her brows. "I worry you may think bad of me for wanting as much."

He didn't have any answers. "I don't think that, Hannah. I won't tell you I haven't kept you on my mind day and night though, since kissing you before."

She touched a finger to his lips. "I know, I think of it too...of us."

"Us?" He questioned as he touched a free strand of her hair.

"Is that what is happening?" She smiled, her blue eyes clear and sure.

"Yeah..." He drew her to him again and this time placed his lips to hers and hugged her tight against him. She clung to him for a moment of breaths, his chest so full of warmth, something he'd long since thought he'd lost. And he held her as tight as he dared, not ever wanting to let go.

****

From the edge of the tree line, Patch Jackson sat his mount, allowing a scowl to cross his face. He'd expected as much. He'd ridden out in the wee hours of the morning and looked on as the day had transpired.

So Sully was teaching Hannah's son to trap and tan hides. He'd seen them both this morning along the river and followed them back to her homestead, where he'd been for a few hours.

Below outside the barn, Sully made chase with the little girl as the boy worked on stretching a hide. Their laughter reached him as he watched, making his anger climb. Hannah was his, or at least she would be, though she'd been quick to thwart the idea of him. He'd had his sights on her since long before her husband's death. She was a handsome and strong woman, even if she had challenged him at the saloon. Well, once he had her where he wanted her, she'd learn not to put him on the spot. He didn't take very kind to a woman's challenge, and she needed to learn her place and at the same time understand she would accept his intentions of her.

And it would be a short time before he'd taught Sully the lesson he needed too. The Johnny Reb had been nothing but trouble. Always challenging for better prices. He never paid for any drink save coffee or sarsaparilla. What kind of man didn't partake of the drink? Well, the man had his coming and soon enough, because he was Patch Jackson, and he didn't lose the things he wanted...ever. And he wanted Hannah Tate, and he would have her too.

Chapter Twelve

Darkness closed in around the cabin as Hannah checked on Gertie and Henry. Both had been sleeping for hours now. Behind her, Sully stood from the table stretching his back, raising his arms above his head. He was so tall; his fingertips grazed the low ceiling there. He'd stayed for a meal after helping with repairs inside the barn.

"All asleep?" He went to the door for his coat and hat. "I'll head out."

She folded her arms, walking closer. "It's so late, and you've no horse."

He smiled and leaned to kiss her cheek. "Walking's good for a man, the darkness too. Never sleep well anyway, like I said. Still hear the gunfire and cannons at times."

"You suffer a soldier's heart, as they say?" She moved closer...somehow wanting to ease what he suffered.

"A soldier's melancholy for a bit, but the dreams fade at times." He shrugged on his coat, and yet she reached out to stop him.

His deep brown eyes held her, and he hung the garment again, his gaze asking what she wasn't sure she could explain, other than it had been so long...so very long since she'd been held and loved. And would this be the evils of sin...to invite him into her bed?

He shook his head. "Hannah?"

"Stay." She took his hand. "Even if for tonight."

He smiled that easy smile that made her heart race. "Hannah, I'll stay one day, but…we both need time to make sure things are right."

"I suppose, but…Sully, I can't eat, I wake thinking of you, as if I'm a smitten schoolgirl once more." She clung to his hand. "You're right, I know you are, but I so want to rush things, to find the *us* we spoke of."

"And we will." He kissed her and reached for his coat again and then turned to hold her gaze. "All right?"

She smiled because she'd grown to love this man in a very short time and now her life seemed to hold the promise of hope. A tomorrow that she would cherish. "Yes. I'm all right."

"That's my girl…" He added his hat and lifted his rifle, opening the door and glancing back at her once more before closing it.

Hannah's entire body was flushed with the feeling of love, of knowing the hope of love and wanting it now. But he was right, waiting was best for a time. She took a deep breath and though she smiled, holding onto the promises that filled her heart.

****

Sully stepped outside into the snow, the cold night filling his lungs with a sting of frozen air. His heart raced at the memory of Hannah asking him to stay. Damn. And he wanted her something fierce. He took a few steps toward the two-mile walk home and then stopped.

Why had he not followed his heart in staying? She'd been clear in her request. What the hell was he afraid of in loving her? He stepped closer again. Hell,

Sarah was gone and no matter the happenings of his life that was not going to change. And it was the same for Hannah. Her husband wasn't coming back.

He turned and glanced at her home and in that instant, cursed with a smile that fed his soul. "Son of a bitch."

He went back to the front door and pushed it open, mindful the children slept and wanting to keep it that way.

Hannah turned, her eyes wide at being startled by him. "Sully?"

"I changed my mind," he whispered, his body already hard and wanting.

She bent to blow out the candle on the table as he set his gun aside and hung his coat and hat. His pulse raced at what was about to happen. He continued to hold her gaze, uncertain as how to go about things. But then she walked to him and took his hand, easing his nerves. He'd been a young man when he'd been with Sarah, and now years had passed.

She led him inside the room to her bed, where they stood for a long moment as she took the pins from her hair before the small mirror. He moved in behind her, lifting a tendril of her brown hair, a loose strand that fell across her shoulder. He held it to the skin of his lips and then inhaled the lilac. "So soft..."

"You remember her like I remember him." Hannah leaned into him, her voice less than a whisper and the warmth of her intoxicating him further.

He turned her and touched her chin, lifting to make her look at him, her blue eyes dark centers wide in the single flame of the small lamp. "No, I want this to be you, Hannah. You and me. It's time for us both...just

91

us."

She took his lips in a tender kiss and lingered until he urged her to open, a soft sigh escaping her. It was as it should be, as they both wanted, and they'd known this early on.

He tasted her and let his hands tug at her blouse, easing it from inside her skirt. He washed a palm over her breasts through her stays, wanting to curse them.

She made haste in untying and letting them fall away. His hands found their blissful want of her breasts, her nipples rising to his touch. It was him who growled then.

Hannah took his hand and led him to the bed and turned back the top covers. She held his gaze as she began with the buttons of her blouse until it fell open.

He touched the garment, tugging until it fell away and then she removed her stays. His breath held heavy as he bent to put his lips to the first breast. He teased and suckled for a time, relishing in her slight moans.

"Want your skin against mine." He pulled free of his shirt and let it drop to the floor. He tugged her closer, and her skin prickled in the cool as he teased a hand to her breast once more, tasting her lips again. His breath went short as she eased a palm across the scar on his shoulder, but when she placed her lips there, he could scarce breathe.

"This is where you were shot?" she whispered, letting her fingers touch tender ease.

He nodded and sucked in a shuddered breath as her lips moved from there to his chest. She ducked her gaze again and slid her hands lower and worked the belt of his trousers. He smiled and stopped her, taking mind to loosen her skirt and the garments underneath, drawing them all down at once.

His breath caught with her naked before him. As beautiful as he'd seen any woman. He kissed her, placing a hand to her jaw and neck. "It's been a long time, Hannah."

"For me as well." She played her hands across the muscles of his chest and kissed the center.

Sully eased her back until she helped herself onto the bed, settling into the pillows, her legs together. He ran a hand from the curve of her breast down her side to her hip. Then to her thigh, allowing him to glimpse the dark patch of curls between her thighs. He looked at her as he let his hands rest behind both knees, moving her legs apart as he watched her.

He bent and kissed her, pushing his trousers down and off as he played his tongue to hers in a heated dance. He lay next to her and traced his hand to her center. She sighed as he rubbed into the slick warmth of her, pressing his fingers inside her depths.

She closed her eyes as he worked her for a time, her hips moving with his efforts, knowing what she desired. He played his mouth at each of her nipples in turn and relished in her hands tangling into his hair as if urging him to more.

Yes, and he'd have more but not until he'd pleased her. He curled his fingers, reaching deeper and her moans filled the room. And then he joined her, hard and searing and began the steady pump of his hips. He growled as she moved with him clinging and rocking as he held her. And when she cried, he covered her mouth with his, wanting to taste her passion. And only when she stilled did he move again, allowing his own hard release. He groaned into her neck and shuddered,

Hannah holding him tighter.

He collapsed into her, brushing her hair back to kiss her again. Her chest rose and fell as hard as his own. But as much as he wanted to hold her all night, it was late, and he couldn't be here when the children woke. He didn't move from her but kissed her lips, chin, cheeks, and then her forehead. Love was his once again. Something he never thought he'd have again in his lifetime. He held her gaze, and she rubbed her hand into the muscles of his back.

He eased from her and tugged her to him, closing his eyes and not wanting to let her go. The feel of her warm body across him was something he'd never take for granted. "I'll have to leave soon."

She shook her head. "Hold me a bit longer."

"Hannah, what if…? You could be with child." He would be happy if that were the case, but with the fact they weren't married, that could be a bad thing for her.

She lifted her head and placed a fingertip to his lips stopping him. "We can't be sure of that now."

He wrapped his arms around her, and she rested against his chest again. "I would do the right thing."

"I know," she whispered and the silence found them again. He closed his eyes, smelling the lilac in her hair and holding her tighter lest a bit of sleep took him from her.

Chapter Thirteen

Hannah smiled as Sully took her hand and brought it to his lips. He kissed her palm as he rolled to his back beside her.

"Gertie is right," he whispered. "I am the man she thinks me…the gingerbread man."

Hannah turned to her side, touching him with the full length of her body and kissed his shoulder. Lands, his loving of her had brought her near tears, it had been so very beautiful. "Why do you say this now?"

He smoothed the hair back from her face. "Because I've…I haven't been truthful on my intentions toward you."

She lifted her gaze, the flame of the small lamp glowed across half his face as he spoke. What was he saying, if he hadn't been truthful? Her breath held.

"I have to tell you…Gertie saw me a few times, but I've been doing things here and there around the homestead for a long time now." He spoke slow and sure, not as if he was falling into guilt from his actions.

"I hadn't known that," she whispered, though somehow she remained calm in his embrace.

He took a deep breath and tangled his hand with hers as he went on. "When…I saw you would be alone with children…" He shrugged. "It was easy to see you'd needed a bit of help…and…all these years I still think if someone had of helped her…helped Sarah…the course of things might have been different, though I wouldn't change them now."

She glanced at their tangled hands. "I am grateful for all you have done...and that you told me. But what of us...this..."

He blinked and kissed her hand again. "This...belongs to us..."

"Yes...but...you said your intentions are clear." She spoke softer. "And what are those things you speak of?"

"Hannah...I've watched from afar...for a long damn time. I don't want to watch anymore...I want to be...with you...and be what I can be to your children." He stopped, tears welling in his eyes. He wanted to curse emotions he couldn't control.

She bit her bottom lip fighting her emotions. Her heart had melted into his words, the fact that she had once more found love. And he did love her, didn't he?

"I've little to offer you other than my hard work, providing what I can...working hard for the rest of it." He shook his head. "I know how short life can be, and so do you and for that may we never forget...but I also know what it means to be lonesome...wishing for something or someone to share...the nights like this, the happy and sad times...the good and bad...all of it."

She wiped a tear that escaped her lashes. "I think that's perhaps the most beautiful words I've ever heard...For the longest time I've been the same. Oh, I know much less time than...when you lost Sarah. But these two years...it's as if I have gone through life each day trying to survive but not living it...and you come along and..."

She brushed away another tear. "And my children

are laughing and playing…you've taught me it's all right to laugh again…love once more."

"Marry me, Hannah…in the spring under the willows…with flowers in your hair and a beautiful dress…" He placed a palm to her cheek, but he didn't wipe the tears that adorned his own. "Let me make you happy for all the days we have."

"Yes." The whisper escaped her though her voice didn't follow because he placed his lips to hers once more.

****

Hannah opened her eyes, not wanting to leave the warmth of her bed. She reached a hand where Sully had been, and he wasn't there. She lifted the edge of the sheet and inhaled the slight lingering scent of him left there.

She'd forced herself not to think of Lucas, even now pushing his face from her mind. Lucas was gone and what was the harm any longer of finding love with Sully?

She hadn't planned at all to fall in love with him. Sully had loved her well into the night, more than once yielding her body to the bliss of their coupling. His words of love had held her as well, as she'd clutched him when his body had given way to his passion.

And now Sully had gone, without a doubt to keep the children from finding him still there. Making her way to the front room, she eased the door back and grabbed the bucket and returned inside to the container of fresh water. Filling the bucket, she went to the stove and poured water into the largest kettle and took time to light the stove. The water would take a bit to warm. She shivered and lit the small lamp on the table but left the flame low in order not to wake the children as she intended to bathe.

When it was ready, she ran the warm water over her body, remembering Sully's touch and blushing at the thought. He'd been thorough with purpose, teasing her into the frenzy of bliss she'd missed for so long. And she'd led him there to her bed without remorse, without dread, with thoughts of it being them alone.

She finished her bathing and dried herself, dressing earlier than usual. Maybe this was a good morning to make more cookies and to talk with the children about her and…Sully. About a future for them all.

"Mama." Gertie walked to her, rubbing her eyes.

She bent and hugged her daughter. "It's early yet, why don't I tuck you back in for a bit so you can stay warm? The sun's not even up for a long while."

Her daughter took her hand with a nod, and she led her back into her smaller room and placed her on the bed under the heavy blankets. "Sleep some more while Mama starts some johnnycakes and bacon for a bit later."

Gertie nodded. "Yes'm."

Hannah began to hum, the easy tune of the same song her mother had raised her on.

"Mama, I saw another gingerbread man in the dark. He waked me up." Gertie glanced at the window. "In the dark on the other side of the barn."

She shook her head. "Gertie, another man?"

"Yes'm, he's a big gingerbread man, not Mr. Sully." Gertie pulled on the blankets with a wide yawn taking her breath. "And he's got a bandage on his eye like Mr. Jackson in town."

"Gertie, when did you see the man?" Hannah

glanced at the small window across the room, her pulse bounding at what this meant. They were not alone.

"He waked me up a minute ago...he sure did." Her daughter snuggled back down into the blankets closing her eyes. "Can I have a cookie when I get up?"

Hannah stood, the hair on the back of her neck rising in fear. "After your breakfast. Go back to sleep, sweetie."

Hannah moved to the window to close the curtain. The bit of light from the small lamp on the kitchen table was all there was as she eased from her daughter's room to peek in on Henry. She opened his door and her heart stopped. His bed lay unmade and a quick glance across to the front door proved he'd taken his hat, coat, and gloves. She must have slept through him and Sully leaving the house. Henry would be out to his traps, but something wasn't right. She glanced at the front door and the bar was up. She stepped toward the table, reaching to dim the lamp, but then someone grabbed her. She screamed.

"I've been nice all along, nice enough to give you a bit of time since your husband's untimely demise." Patch Jackson chuckled in a growl, whisky lacing his breath and his cold hand on her.

Hannah froze as he held a gun in one hand and now her in the other. "What are you doing here?"

"I've come for what's going to be mine." He whispered his words hard at her ear. "That's right, I've seen him here, and it ends now because you will be mine, Hannah. All mine."

He pushed her to the table. Slamming her across it and raising her skirts. No, he couldn't...She tried to fight, but he turned her and slapped a fist across her face. She was knocked backward as another fist caught her brow. Her head spun and for a moment she was confused.

He came at her again, and she ducked to miss the hit. He grabbed her by her loose hair and dragged her back to the table. "I've played fair, Hannah, waiting, but not anymore, and when I'm done here, he's gonna pay as well." He slammed her down again, working the front of his belt, his breath hard.

"You can't do this." She tried to push him away, but he had her pinned. As she recalled, trying to make sense of things, she'd never been hit before. She pushed back from the table, and he jerked her around again, grabbing her by the neck.

"Oh, but sweets, I sure can. I run this town, and all who are in it. You should know that by now." He growled as he squeezed. "Or at least you will."

Hannah placed both hands to his trying to breathe, throwing the heel of her hand to catch his chin. His head popped back, but then he gave an evil smile.

"Mama..." Gertie stood at her door.

Hannah crumbled to the floor, holding her stomach, rasping to inhale a breath.

"Get outta here, go on!" Patch yelled at her daughter.

"Mama...Mommy..." The little girl squatted down in the corner, clutching her doll.

Patch grabbed Hannah and dragged her to the table once more, lifting her skirts. She swung both her balled fists.

But then he was on her, pinning her to the table and shoving her skirts higher. His slap found the side of her face twice more, and she lost consciousness for a moment, Gertie's shrill screams bringing her back. She tried to move as he gripped her thigh.

No…she fought again but another fist came and another. She screamed with what was left inside her lungs. "Run, Gertie…run."

But then another hit came, and her words wouldn't come. Jackson let her go, and she slid to the floor, unable to hold herself standing. Aware of the scuffle behind her, she began to crawl toward Gertie along the floor. Reaching her, she couldn't form the words to speak, her mind confused. She rested her hand to her daughter and closed her eyes as the blackness invaded her mind, Gertie fading from her view.

Chapter Fourteen

Sully slammed a fist across Patch Jackson's cheek. The man, twice his size, shoved him backwards. He righted himself and lunged again, taking them both to the ground. He'd gotten back to his cabin to find it in disarray and had returned to check on Hannah and the children, suspecting as much. His intuitions had been right as Patch Jackson had been attacking Hannah.

He'd arrived to Gertie crying and Hannah's screams. He had bolted through the front door. There he'd found Patch Jackson beating Hannah, having her pinned to the table with his body.

"You bastard." Jackson clawed into him, scrambling for the pistol lying on the floor. Sully kicked and the weapon slid further away as a fist caught his brow. He wrestled to reach the knife in his boot, but Jackson was too strong, and a knee found his side. He coughed for breath.

He fought for position and punched twice, catching the man's jaw, but Jackson still came back.

"Told you, Johnny Reb, you need to leave my town." The man's fist caught his brow, and he fell back, though Jackson followed. But the gun was in reach and Jackson grabbed it and cocked the weapon before he could free himself.

Sully froze, his vision blurred and across the room Hannah didn't move as Gertie screamed and cried, clinging to her mother.

"Well, this is fine…let's you and me walk outside and finish this." Patch made it to his feet, holding the weapon to him. "Right now, or I'll shoot them both right here and you to follow. I always win, Sully. You should've learned that by now. Move."

Sully glanced at Hannah who began to moan. What in the hell had this bastard done?

"Now!" Patch yelled, and Gertie's intensity of screaming cries increased, the little girl breathless in her fright.

Sully stood, tasting blood. His vision was blurred from a hit. He staggered on purpose buying time. Jackson would kill him no doubt, and there were few seconds to think about what he might try.

"Walk, Sullivan, and it might be I'll be quick about it, spare the little girl watching." Jackson motioned with the pistol, and he walked to the door and out onto the porch. The best he had was to make a run for it, but then the bastard would hurt Hannah and Gertie anyway.

He moved straight and then the whistle came in the early morning dawn. Henry. *Son of a bitch!* The last thing he needed was Henry coming home in the middle of this fight.

Jackson glanced out into the woods as they both left the porch. "Boy, I know you're out there, come out, and I won't hurt you or your mother or that little sister of yours."

The darkness of morning remained as it was.

"No, Henry, stay where you are." Sully yelled and Jackson brought the butt of the pistol across the back of his head. He dropped to his knees in the snow, senseless. He had to fight, but when?

Jackson waved the pistol, shouting. "Boy, you come out of the woods right now or when I find you, I'll gut you like one of those animals you trap."

Still nothing.

Sully gripped snow into his fists. All he had would be a quick jump up and slinging of the ice and a scramble to fight before a bullet found him.

"Last chance, boy." Jackson yelled again across the whiteness of the morning. "I'll find you…but first, you watchin', huh? You watching, boy?"

The man lowered the pistol and let it rest against the back of Sully's head. "You should have left this town a while back, Johnny Reb. I've warned you over and over."

Sully didn't move, waiting for the impact. Patch would kill him no doubt, and he only had one shot at turning the cards. He jumped around and slung the ice in his hands toward the man's face. Jackson stumbled back a step and then poised the pistol once more.

Sully gulped as Patch's finger tightened on the trigger. He waited and somehow as the blast sounded, he never felt the impact or the burn. He opened his eyes, and Patch Jackson stumbled backward, the ice crunching under his boots and the pistol dropping in the snow as the man fell.

What the hell had happened? Sully grabbed the pistol from the ground, aiming at Jackson and shooting twice more. The giant of a man moved but then fell dead. He glanced behind him. In the distance, Henry lowered the smoking shotgun.

"It's all right, Henry, we hadn't a choice." Sully nodded at the boy, proud of him somehow.

Gertie's screams found them both, and the boy ran

to him and fell against him, bursting into tears. "Ma and Gertie?" Henry wiped his eyes and glanced at the house. "He was gonna kill all of us...Ma?"

"Come on. I think she's all right." Sully took off on a run toward the home, his heart in his throat in wondering if Hannah was all right. He burst through the doorway, and Gertie screamed louder, crouched in the corner.

Henry ran to Hannah, who still lay on the floor, though she moaned, holding her face. "Ma...Mama?"

She tried to sit but then lay back down. "I'm...fine...Henry...I'm all right. Gertie..." She reached for her daughter, who crowded further into the corner away from her.

Sully bent and lifted the little girl. "Shhhh, it's all right. He's all gone now. He's all gone." The little girl clung to him, and he'd never felt a child shake so hard.

He grabbed a blanket and wrapped her in it, as she continued to sob. "Henry, take your sister so I can see to your mama. Here, go to Henry, I gotta help Mama."

Henry nodded, his face distorted in tears. He took his sister and held her, rocking and shushing her while he stood. "Will Ma be all right?"

Sully bent and gathered Hannah into his arms. "I think so..."

"I'm fine." She tried to resist but then allowed him to carry her to her bed.

Hannah looked at him, one eye swollen shut. "How did you know?"

Sully shook his head. "Don't talk. Rest."

Henry sat in the chair outside the door rocking Gertie and talking to her. "It's all right, Gertie, I got you. It's all over. He won't bother us ever again."

Sully pulled the covers over Hannah and went to the basin on the side table. He poured water from the pitcher and added a rag. He wrung it and sat on the side of the bed placing the cool rag to her swollen brow and eye.

She moaned but placed her hand with his. "Gertie?"

He nodded, glancing at Henry and his sister, who was quiet now. "She's all right, frightened, Henry is holding her."

His own hands were shaking with the nerves of the fight and his worry for Hannah. He gritted his teeth at what Jackson had done. but Hannah opened her one eye to look at him.

"Are you all right...where do you hurt?" Sully asked, it would take him an hour or more to get to town and return with the doctor. "I'll let Henry sit with you and go for the doc."

She shook her head. "Time to rest is all I need."

His heart was racing, and he wasn't sure what to do. He moved the rag to clean the blood from her lip and cheek, all the while Hannah watching him. "Hannah, he didn't...I mean...he..."

She shook her head once more. "No, he tried...but you came. Where is he?"

"He won't bother you anymore, Hannah, but you need a doctor, in case." He touched her cheek, and she winced.

"Sully?" Her good eye widened. "He took you out to shoot you, and I couldn't get up and..." She broke into tears "I thought..."

"Shhh, had the finest marksman in the woods on my side," he answered as Henry brought in Gertie and laid his sleeping sister beside their mother.

"We got him, Ma...didn't have a choice, but me and Sully got him together." Henry glanced from him to his mother, though the boy's tears were evident.

Hannah laid her hand to her son's arm and pulled him closer. "Henry, I'm so sorry..."

"No, Ma, he was gonna kill Sully and all of us, but we got him, me and Sully together." The boy held a sense of pride as he crawled onto the bed beside her.

Sully smiled at the picture. Hannah and her children safe. Shaken up but safe. He continued to clean her face. She was without a doubt the strongest most beautiful woman he'd ever encountered.

"You look so tired," she whispered, as Henry had closed his eyes.

He nodded and lifted her hand to show her the bruises there. "Fighting is hard work, as you know."

She gritted her teeth. "Indeed."

He kissed her hand and laid it back beside her. "I'll go take care of things, bring back the doctor like I said. I won't be long."

She took his hand in hers. "Thank you, Sully."

He leaned to kiss the top of her head. "Took me a long time to find you, wasn't about to let you go so soon."

Chapter Fifteen

Hannah pulled the plum pudding from the heavy iron stove and sat it to cool. She fought with the broken door to get it open and then shut again. Behind her, the children were cutting out cookies. The storm outside blew with brisk winds and heavy snows, bringing in another unexpected blizzard. Sully had gone to sell the pelts and hides he and Henry had ready, but he hadn't returned yet. It was Christmas Eve, and he should have been back by now, though it was the weather that had delayed him.

She supposed she'd be happy that he'd taken Henry a week ago out to find the tree that adorned the corner of the room, scant with the few gifts. But she had so wanted to share the time of Christmas with Sully. She sighed.

"Gertie, all the gingerbread men aren't supposed to look like Sully," Henry scolded, glancing outside into the evening darkness, sulking to himself over not being able to go with Sully.

Her daughter brushed back the hair from her face. "Well, Sully is the bestest gingerbread man in the whole wide world. He save-ded Mama and me from that bad man."

"I helped too, I's the one who…"

"Henry." Hannah stopped him, shaking her head. Talking about what had happened to them all a few weeks back wasn't what needed to be discussed at Christmas. It had been a lot to take in, a lot to understand, and both children had slept with her for the last days since. As it was, they'd all been able to put the event behind them. She had Sully to thank for that. He'd come by each day and played with the children and helped her with chores. She'd healed, though the bruising might take a bit longer.

And while Sully hadn't returned, she smiled anyway. Gertie had clapped, and Henry had even offered a smile. So, when spring came, she would once again be a married woman.

"Well, I like Sully, and the brown gingerbread mans taste like lots of sugar." Gertie licked her fingers with a smack of her lips. "And I am leaving this biggest one for Santa Claus tonight 'cause he'll bring my dolly when I waked up in the morning. And Henry Lucas Tate, if you haven't been a good boy, he's gonna leave you nothing but a big sack of coal."

"Ma..." Henry rolled his eyes and glanced at her, annoyed.

"Gertie, that isn't very nice, now," Hannah scolded with a lift of her brows.

"Yes'm." Gertie sprinkled more sugar across the cookies, though she batted her eyes at her brother.

Henry eyed her, well aware that the doll had been out of her price range and the dress she'd made hadn't sold. Well, at least she had finished the shirt for him and Gertie's smock. They would have candy and an orange in their stockings but not much more.

"I want you both to wash up when you're done tonight. We'll have milk and cookies, and tomorrow our Christmas ham with yams and biscuits and green beans. But first, Henry…" She looked at her son who lifted his gaze. "I want you to light the star on the tree and all the candles like your pa always did."

His blue eyes were wide for a moment. "Yes'm. But you wanted to wait on Sully."

"Well, I'm afraid with the storm he's delayed." She walked closer and picked up Gertie to watch as Henry took a twig of flame form the hearth to begin lighting the candles with intentional care. He'd grown so much the last year, and there were times he caught a hint of Lucas. She supposed her late husband would have been proud of him with all that had happened.

"Henry Lucas Tate, I do believe that's as pretty a tree as ever I did see." Gertie giggled and hugged her, her daughter's comment making them all laugh until a loud thud on the porch sounded.

"The boogeyman." Gertie whimpered and clung to her frightened.

"It's all right. It may be a limb or something that has fallen with the weather, I'm sure." She moved toward the window to look outside, though Henry beat her there.

"It's Sully, Ma. It's Sully."

****

Sully steadied himself, as he stood in the doorway of Hannah's home. He smiled, though he couldn't feel his face. Maybe he should have known better, but he'd made it through one of the worst blizzards he'd ever encountered.

"Sully, you're near frozen." Hannah sat Gertie down and pulled him inside and closed the door behind him. Winds whipped all the way to the fireplace hearth as he shivered and inhaled the scent of sugar and spice.

"Cold…" It was the one word he could manage for the time being.

Hannah and Henry helped him out of the ice-covered buffalo robe he'd worn to stay warm. He made a mental note to pay attention to the sky the next time he thought he'd have a quick jaunt north for selling his pelts.

"Sully, you're almost a snowman." Henry took his hat and pulled the heavy frozen mitts off each of his hands.

He glanced at them, making as much a fist as he could with his cold hands. Ice fell from his shirt and trousers. "The…th…the coat will drip when…it warms." He warned Hannah, his teeth chattering as he spoke.

"Nothing I cannot get right up," she said, her bright blue eyes smiling, though he was sure any minute he might collapse of exhaustion if he thought hard about it. He'd been at it for miles and miles, including a quick jaunt to town. He'd placed Sage and Sampson inside Hannah's barn, and it seemed the last few steps to the house were the longest, but he'd made it.

"How'd you get here in this?" Henry asked as he sat, allowing the boy to pull each of his boots from his nearly frozen feet.

"See, he's the gingerbread man…see." Gertie picked up one of the cookies, and it might have been he was a true match. She ran to him and handed the cookie to him.

"I suppose I do look the part in this." He held Hannah's gaze and then moved closer to the fire, his clothing covered in ice as he sat on the hearth. He took a bite of the cookie, reveling in the feeling of it hitting the bottom of his empty belly.

"Did you see Santa Claus out there in the dark? He's gonna comed down our chimney and leave us presents tonight." Gertie swirled to make her dress flap around her, making him grin.

He squeezed his thawing hands open and closed and glanced at Hannah. Damn if she wasn't the sight he needed, more of a beauty every time he saw her.

He turned back to Gertie. "I tell ya, I did see someone, mind you."

The little girl's eyes widened as he spoke. "Henry bring my pack there."

Henry did as he was asked and lifted the sack, handing it to him, kneeling to the floor before him. He first lifted paper money from his shirt pocket. "Here's your...money for the hides you had."

Henry took the rolled bills and counted. "Sixteen dollars, Ma. Thank you, Sully."

Hannah came closer, handing him a towel and she pulled one of the chairs beside him, lifting Gertie to her lap. "That's well more than you expected."

Sully nodded as he used a drying cloth, the ice dripping from his hair as he warmed. His hands were numb and pounded in pain as they came back to life. He made a fist several more times. "Well, you see...I got back from selling the hides, not an easy ride in the blizzard, but I had to drop pelts in town and then I headed here. But it was hard as the dickens to see in that snow and the dark, but I come up over the rise and that's when I seen him..."

"Santa Claus," Gertie whispered, her eyes wide with wonder.

Sully nodded. "I'd a mind to check on you all, but

then I saw him, walking along with a bigger sack than I've ever seen. I thought about turning back, giving up, but then I kept hearing bells in the distance and decided to follow what he was up to."

"Santa Claus, you seen him…" Gertie cuddled into her mother, but it was Henry who was as interested, with his mouth held open.

"Well, I followed him to the clearing, and Sage and Sampson made a bit too much noise and he turned to see me standing there." He held Hannah's gaze as she smiled and listened as well.

"He sized me up for a long minute and says…'Say, feller, you think you could help me a little? Seems my reindeer and sleigh got a bit away from me with the winds but they're up ahead.' And he pointed." Sully wiped the towel over his damp face and beard.

"What happened then?" This time it was Henry who asked, scooting closer.

"Well, I was a bit nervous, Santa Claus likes everything to be a secret and he says, 'Where you headed this evening in the likes of this blizzard?' I told him I needed to visit to check on things here at the homestead and he says, 'Gertie and Henry Tate?' And I say, 'Yes, that's them.' "

"Santa knows us like I done thought," Gertie whispered, her voice rising an octave.

"Sure, he does, he knew my name too, said, 'Say, aren't you John Sullivan there, Sully?'

"I say, 'Yes, that's me, Sir.'" He smiled trying to make it all animated for the children. "And he says, 'This storm has the reindeer a bit frazzled, never even seen the likes of this at the North Pole. I'd be obliged if you might take these gifts to Gertie and Henry for me.

I'm a mite late and need to get us back on schedule.' "

"What happened then?" Gertie fidgeted in her mother's lap.

Hannah met his gaze with a smile of satisfaction as Henry moved even closer to him.

"Well, I of course told him I could bring the things, but then he said, 'Remind the children of minding their ma and sayin' their prayers and all.' And he tossed this sack here to me, and then it was the darndest thing I ever did see. I followed him to the clearing like I said, and there it was, the biggest snow sleigh I ever did see with bells all over it. And before I could say thank you, he and those reindeer were gone in the blink of my eyes with a loud bump in the night." He blinked hard to illustrate the point.

"That must be what we heard we heard hit the house." Henry again, his eyes wide with wonder.

"It sure tossed snow and ice all over me, if I wasn't covered enough. Thought I might freeze to death before I could get here, but Sage and Sampson saved me. They're in your barn now," Sully explained, using the towel on his damp hair.

Gertie's hands were each on her cheeks and her mouth open. "What did Santa send us?"

Henry's gaze was glued to him too. "What's in the sack, can we, Ma?"

"Well, I suppose since Santa came a bit early, but your other gifts and stockings must wait until after our Christmas meal tomorrow," Hannah answered the children though she held his gaze. She couldn't know what he'd done, and he hoped she'd accept what he'd brought for her and the children.

"Well, let's see how things go." He lifted the sack

and dug inside and pulled free a small wrap and handed one each to the children. "Go ahead…"

Henry pulled free a fat peppermint stick. "Look, Ma."

"I got one too." Gertie giggled and gave the striped wand a lick.

Sully took out the wooden box he'd been the most careful with and sat it before her. "Santa said to be careful carrying this one for Gertie because she'd been such a good girl this year."

"All mine…" The little girl admired the box and glanced at her mother. "May I opened it up, Mama?"

Hannah nodded, leaning closer to her. "Yes, but be very careful."

Gertie pulled up the lid, Henry helping her by setting it aside.

"Oh, Mama, see, Santa Claus remembered." Gertie took up the silk-dressed China doll and hugged her, rocking back and forth. "Oh, mama. She's the prettiest ever."

Hannah met his gaze, her eyes glistening. Well, he hadn't meant to bring her tears, but he suspected they were the happy kind.

He smiled a little, hoping for the next gift he'd find a bit of forgiveness. He looked at Henry. "Santa said I'z to leave yours outside till time, but I suspect now is time. It's leaning beside the door. Watch the winds."

Henry's mouth dropped open, and he trotted to the door, flinging it open. He returned a moment later slamming it behind him. In his hand was a shiny new shotgun. "Ma, look, it's a shotgun like in town." The boy held the shiny new weapon with caution and curiosity.

Hannah looked from Henry to him and back. "I suppose you're old enough now."

"Oh, well, Santa said it wasn't loaded, but I do think…" Sully dug into the sack again. "It came with a box of these, knew something was heavy in the pack."

Henry walked over, carrying the shotgun and took the box of shells. "I've never had such a nice gift and all." The boy sat in the chair at the table and opened the carton to view the metal shotgun shells stacked inside. "Twenty, Ma…I can hunt when this clears."

"Oh, I do worry, you must be careful," Hannah warned, though she still smiled.

"I will, Ma. I promise." Henry ran a hand across the stock, admiring the shiny new weapon. It had set him back a good bit, but the boy deserved his own gun after all they had been through. He'd never seen a braver boy in his life.

"I'll practice with him some when the weather clears. We can site the gun and make sure it's accurate." Sully tried to smooth things over. "There's a little something more though."

Hannah angled a glance at him as he lifted the brown paper wrap from inside the large sack and handed it to her.

"Mama, Santa got you something too!" Gertie jumped up and down holding her doll and waiting beside her mother.

"Oh, my, well…" Hannah took the package he gave to her, but she looked at him. "Sully…"

"Go on." He urged her with a nod.

"Yes, well, I…" She opened the brown paper with care. "Why, I…" She placed a hand to her mouth.

"Ma, it's the dress you made, the one for sale."

Henry held the box of bullets.

"Santa must have buyed it." Gertie added her thoughts, recognizing the garment as well.

He'd made the purchase of it since it hadn't sold, but he didn't want it to sell. He wanted to see Hannah wear it for herself.

"I see." Her voice cracked. "Sully. It never sold, maybe because part of me wished it hadn't."

"Don't thank me, Santa has a mind for what was needed." Sully shrugged, though the smile on her sweet face made it all worth his trouble. He looked on as she stood and shook the dress free, measuring it against her.

Gertie touched the fine dress. "Mama, you can wear it tomorrow all day for Christmas."

"That I can." She spoke and held his gaze, hanging the dress on her door. It didn't go past him that she wiped her eyes before turning back to them all.

"Like I said, that Santa fellow was in a great hurry. Must have ran through town earlier before those reindeer started kicking up trouble." Sully made excuses as the children went about with their gifts, Gertie dancing with her doll and Henry glancing to site the empty shotgun.

"I know it's early and all, but I wanted to make sure like Santa asked I got the things here. But I've a mind if I don't leave soon, I may as well freeze on the trek home." He stood, glad for the time to give them the gifts but not wanting to head back to his home, darn blizzard.

Hannah shook her head. "You can't go in this; we'll make you a bed near the hearth."

"I wouldn't want to impose..." He said it as he glanced at the fire. He'd come so they'd have the gifts but stayin', well, not in her bed would be a tough one.

"Nonsense, right children?" She folded her arms as if she'd scold him.

"Yeah." Gertie ran and wrapped her arms around him. "You're the gingerbread man, and you will freeze so you have to stay. And eat cookies and open presents in the morning and eat cake and play with us, Sully." The little girl danced around him.

"Yeah, we can maybe site my gun tomorrow if the weather lessens," Henry added, laying the gun along the table.

Sully met Hannah's gaze and gave a nod. Well, he could make it on the floor by the hearth a night or two. But soon enough and with the children's permission, he was gonna share a bed with Hannah for the rest of his life. Anything to be near her and to make sure every breath she took was a happy one.

He nodded and now was as good as time as any. "There's, uhm…" He'd waited on purpose, though he hadn't planned on tonight. "There is one more small gift, but it's not from Santa Claus."

Hannah watched him as he pulled the small pouch from inside his shirt. He bent to a knee and opened the box before her. He had been going to wait until he returned tomorrow but…

Hannah put her hands to her cheeks. "Sully?"

"I, uh…I'm not so good at fancy words and all. I was saving this for tomorrow, though I think now is as good a time as any." He adjusted and lifted the ring from the pouch. "Hannah, marry me come spring when it's warm again and wear that dress there with flowers in your hair and…make me the happiest man in the whole world."

"Go on, Ma, Sully told me all about it, and it's the way it should be. Won't it make you happy, Ma?" Her son tried to convince her, stepping closer.

She touched the gold band in his hand and Sully placed it on her finger. "Yes, very much."

"Mama, you gotta marry Sully, he's the gingerbread man." Gertie leaned against her mother, hugging her doll.

Hannah glanced at her children and back to him, "Well, I suppose since you are the gingerbread man, I will say yes to your proposal."

With that Sully pulled her close and kissed her for a moment before both children began clapping and hugging them. "Merry Christmas, Hannah…"

"Merriest of Christmases, Sully."

Epilogue

Christmas Day/Morning, 1876

Sully paced across the kitchen floor to the window and glanced outside yet again. He'd been at it for hours, listening, pacing and on the edge of worrying himself damn near to death. The snowfall that had begun early that morning still raged full on, leaving several feet of snow. He and Henry had finished most of the chores earlier that morning. But the day had also started with Hannah in labor, and his race to town to bring Naomi back to the homestead to help her.

He'd been in and out most of the day, at least until the last few hours. That's when Naomi had told him and the children it would still be a while longer, but they were to remain outside for Hannah to have a bit of rest before the baby came. Now all he'd heard for the last hour was mumbling as the ladies talked to each other behind the door.

He supposed he didn't belong in there, but some part of him wanted to be with Hannah, to soothe what part of the pain she had to endure. But Naomi, a fine midwife in her own right, had shut that door.

"Sure does take a long time to have a baby." Henry sat at the table munching on gingerbread cookies Hannah and Gertie had made the day before. Strange in his fatigue, the hours nearing midnight, it seemed like an eternity ago that the table was covered with flour, cookie dough, and decorations of dried fruit, nuts, and icing.

His pulse raced, his patience thinned, and so he walked the floors, again. "I guess babies take their own sweet time, like Naomi said." He supposed he wasn't making Henry feel any better. They were all tired, and across the room, Gertie lay sleeping on the settee. She'd fallen into her slumber hours before, and he'd covered her with a blanket and let her stay where she was, promising to wake her when the baby arrived.

"Well, this one is sure taking its time." Henry gave a wide yawn and laid his head on his folded arms across the table.

Sully pulled the pocket watch from his vest. Twelve. "I'm gonna get Gertie to her bed. Why don't you go on to sleep, get some rest? I'll wake you when the baby's here, I promise."

He lifted Gertie across his shoulder.

"I wanna stay up…see…the baby…too." She plopped her head onto his shoulder and said no more. He chuckled as he laid her into her own small bed and tugged the covers over her, the nightly routine he'd taken up this last year as he'd moved into the house. He laid a hand lightly on her cheek and smiled. It wasn't this new baby that would make him a father. Hannah's children had done that, taking to calling him Pa in a short time after he and Hannah had married. He dimmed the lantern, eased her door closed, and returned to the kitchen.

"She's sleeping already…" He spoke to Henry but stopped. The boy hadn't moved and without a doubt slept where he was. He walked over and laid a hand to his shoulder. "Henry, come on…"

The lad stood without protest and stumbled his way to his room, closing the door behind him. That hadn't taken much, but the excitement of the baby and it being Christmas had given them all a lot to do. Fatigue had long taken him too, though worry for Hannah kept him moving.

He glanced at the doorway again as Hannah gave a cry. Fears rode through his chest. He'd lost a wife and a child once before in his life, and he didn't care to go through that loss again. His breath held, but then her soft remaining moan faded. And so it had been for hours now. He moved to the window again, looking out. The moon lit across the homestead, the place he now lived and the place he loved Hannah and her children—his children. And while it had been a long time since he'd offered any kind of conversation with the God of heaven, he closed his eyes for a time, giving up the silent words of protection.

It had been the early spring he'd married Hannah. The first sun-filled day that had shown them flowers and green grasses. The ceremony had been in the field by the church, with patrons of Harper Falls in attendance. Right under the willows. Gertie had sprinkled flower petals all along the path for Henry to walk his mother to become his wife. It had been the most special day to finally hold Hannah in his arms and know that life was indeed full of surprises he'd never take for granted.

And with Patch Jackson out of the way and for good, the town of Harper Falls had begun to thrive. Businesses were making money, and even Zeke had dried himself out and was running the trading post and saloon at a fair price for all. Hannah and Henry had continued to raise and sell chickens and eggs. With that and what he and Henry had earned in tanning hides, Christmas would mean everyone got a little something they had wanted.

With the children off to bed, he shook his head. He found the hidden sack of gifts to put in the children's stockings. Hannah had worried, but he'd taken on the new role of being Santa. He smiled as he eased a knife he'd made into Henry's stocking and new hair ribbons he'd found on a trip to Cheyenne into Gertie's. And in Hannah's stocking he put a small glass container of lemon verbena and a tin of something she would love—real dried ginger.

He spent the next few hours taking three trips to the barn to bring in the items Hannah had hidden from the children. He'd placed all the gift-wrapped items under the small, decorated tree in the corner. And then he'd rearranged them twice again, thinking Hannah would want it all to look nice.

Keeping himself busy helped, with the children now asleep, and once he was done, he glanced at his pocket watch again. Four in the morning and the snow still blew in droves outside. But it remained quiet behind the door where Hannah labored. One last trip to the barn should do it on the presents.

He eased the door open, careful again not to wake the children, and made his way to the barn in the drifts. He shoved his gloves on his hands and made his way inside to the mooing protests of the old cow Bess.

"Relax, girl, last time I gotta open this door." He sat the lantern he carried on the worktable and eyed the large box in the corner. He'd planned on Henry's help, but they had waited a bit too late. He'd ordered the new stove out of Chicago and kept it hidden in the box, covering it with a heavy canvas he now removed, stirring up dust and straw. The stove Hannah cooked on had seen better days, and he'd repaired it time and again. This new stove wasn't much larger but had all new parts. He scooted the box out and lifted with a grunting heave. He settled it into his arms and made his way back outside into the weather.

The box was almost more than he could manage alone, and he set it to the snow once for a rest. That's when he saw Gertie in the window. He smiled and placed his gloved finger to his lips. She nodded and skipped away. He must have woken her going in and out the door.

He fumbled with it to get the box with the stove to the porch and then inside, scooting it across the kitchen floor as quietly as he could. He eased it into the corner with a satisfied nod. He then stepped to Gertie's door opening it.

She lay back in her bed but smiled. "You got a big box out there, did Santa leave it for you like last time, asking you to help?"

He nodded his head in agreement. "Sure did, a lot of snow blowing out there, and he needed to be on his way."

She sat up, but he moved closer, pulling the covers over her again. Her light hair was in disarray all around her face, but she snuggled in, holding *The Gingerbread Man* book he'd now read about a hundred times.

"Read." She pushed the book his way.

Well, who was he not to do as the lady asked? He sat on the edge of the bed and opened the book. With a deep breath he began reading. He'd no more than hit the first "Run, run, fast as you can, you can't catch me, I'm the gingerbread man," when Gertie closed her eyes. He whispered a line or two more out of memory alone as he stood. He closed the book, careful not to wake her again, setting it aside.

He left the room and headed back out to the barn once more to gather the lantern and bring the last of the items from the barn. No wonder Santa was a tired man, but he suspected Santa hadn't waited this long on a baby before. He settled back inside the house and placed the last of the gifts under the tree with the boxed up stove nearby.

He glanced at the tree and then went to arrange the packages again. Hannah would like things to look nice, and he'd never really worried of such things. Strange he'd never had Christmas with so many gifts since he was a boy. But right now the only gift he needed was Hannah and the baby to be all right.

Hannah gave a cry and another. He turned and waited, shuffling behind the door the first noises he'd heard in a long while. And then came the soft mewling whine of a baby.

He moved toward the door, alarmed as to how much time had passed. The baby was here. "Is…is everything all right?"

From the other side of the door came Naomi's voice. "One minute, Papa…Let me get this baby all wrapped up."

Papa? He smiled, his heart racing. All he could do was stare at the door and wait, his thoughts rambling faster than he could think them. "She's all right then?"

"Well, can't you hear her?" Naomi questioned him

through the door.

"So a girl then?" He smiled, assuming. Happy no matter.

"No, can't you hear your wife? Come on in, Papa." Naomi opened the door and tugged him through.

He met Hannah's gaze, and she smiled, holding the small bundle against her chest.

Somehow, he managed a breath as he stepped closer, having never seen anything more beautiful than his wife. Her hair was braided and hung down her chest. Her blue eyes were clear and showed her fatigue, but he'd keep this picture of her holding their child as long as he lived.

She patted the bed beside her, the baby's soft cries continuing as he sat. He wasn't sure but thought he might even weep, though he fought the urge. She was all right. His Hannah was just fine.

She offered the bundle to him, and he held her gaze as he brought the baby to his embrace and peeked at the tiny face. "So small." He couldn't recall the last time he'd held a baby so tiny or if ever.

"Well, aren't you going to ask?" She smiled, and tugged the blankets back from the infant's face.

He looked at her again and waited.

"A son, Sully, a boy…your son." She placed a hand with his along the baby's head.

"A boy?" He whispered and studied the baby who hushed, sucking his small fingers.

"John then? You never would agree…" She giggled as she'd wanted to choose names long before now and he hadn't been certain for boy or girl what names to decide on.

"I thought he might be a girl, and I'm afraid a girl

wouldn't much like being called John." He eased closer to her as Naomi shut the door and left them to themselves for the moment.

"The children?" she asked. "I tried so hard not to make much noise, but it's no easy feat." She adjusted in the bed to sit up more, leaning against him to look at the baby.

"I promised I'd wake them both. Are you all right?" he asked, though he almost couldn't take his eyes from his son. So it seemed the God in heaven had met his words.

"Oh, I will be with a little rest, Papa." She giggled and then yawned.

Sully brushed a hand across her face. "I worried so…"

"I know you did, and I worried about you too, but I'm fine and we have a son. Gertie may be so upset, she wanted a sister, but now you and Henry will have help around here in a few years." She added, "But Sully, the presents and all for the children…and…"

"Everything's done." He chuckled as he held the small warm bundle. "He's a little thing."

Naomi entered again with a bowl of broth and a spoon. "Actually, he's a big boy, almost nine pounds according to the scale I carry. I woke the children."

Henry appeared at the door carrying a sleepy Gertie. She lifted her head and then climbed from her brother's arms, trotting to the bed. "Mama, the baby's here…it's here…"

The little girl leaned on the edge of the bed trying to see.

"Henry, Gertie, meet your little brother…John." Hannah looked at him and he smiled.

Gertie protested, placing her hands to her hips. "Aw, I wanted a baby sister, not a boy."

Henry only smiled and held his place at the door.

Sully got up and carried the baby to the other side of the bed and bent. "I have a feeling you'll like him well enough."

The little girl's eyes widened as she took a good look at her brother. "Oh, Mama, he is like Clara but a real baby dolly. Can I hold him, can I?"

Hannah nodded. "You can in just a little while, but he's very small and you'll have to sit on the settee."

"I will, Mama…I will sit and hold him all day long for you." The little girl bent to kiss the baby's head. "I think a brother is just fine, I do. And I seen it when Sully, when the gingerbread man bringed him inside. I seen that big box, so it's not like Cammie told me that the stork bird drops new babies to their mamas. Santa must leave them in the barn for the daddies to bring in."

Naomi appeared in the doorway behind Henry. "George is here, Hannah, I'll be back to check on you all in a few days. You've done very well. There's breakfast on the table and a bit of broth on the stove if you don't feel much like the food."

"Thank you, Naomi, and Merry Christmas. Please go on to your family this day." Hannah urged her friend.

Naomi smiled and made her exit from the room, and then a moment later the front door opened and closed.

Sully turned with the baby and walked over to Henry. "Seems you and I've a hunting partner once he's a little bigger."

Henry pulled his hands from his pockets, eyeing

the baby. "He's small. Guess I don't much remember when Gertie was that little."

"You hold him?" Sully eased the baby into Henry's arms. The boy held his brother a bit awkwardly but smiled, the kind of smile Sully liked to see on the boy.

"Hey, how come Henry gets to hold him?" Gertie folded her arms but turned to her mother.

Sully bent to her, hoping to change her focus. "Tell ya what, I'll bet since I seen Santa in the barn last night, those stockings and presents are a waiting right there under the tree. He didn't ask me about anything but that big box, so there's just no telling what we might find."

"Oh, yeah, it's Christmas, I done near forgot." She trotted from the room as Henry made his way over to hand the baby to Hannah.

"I'm glad you're all right, Ma. It took an awful long time." Henry shrugged. "Tried to stay awake and all."

"You needed your sleep, and I am just fine." Hannah tousled his hair, and he eased from the room with a nod.

"You look tired." Sully brushed the hair back from her face as he admired his son. The baby squirmed and began to fuss.

"I'll be all right," she whispered, gazing at the baby and tucking him back into his swaddlings "I think he's hungry. I'll feed him, and you and the children have your breakfast."

He kissed her cheek and watched as she placed the baby to her breast with a practiced ease. He touched the baby's tiny hand, and the little fingers curled around his. "I can't get over how small he is."

"He looks so much of you." Hannah angled a gaze

toward the baby and then back to him.

He shook his head. "I spent a lot of time, a lot of years not thinking I'd ever be happy again. Not thinking I could find a way to keep each day something I wanted. But when I married you, God, Hannah, when I knew you were mine, everything has fallen right into a place I want to be each day."

A tear escaped her, but she spoke anyway. "I only wanted my children to be happy, I never thought it would be mine to find again, but…Oh, Sully isn't he so beautiful? And the children will be happy today."

He took her hand in his and kissed her palm, and leaned closer to kiss John's tiny head.

"It's already morning." She yawned but gave him a smile. "Merry Christmas, Sully."

He leaned in to kiss her softly on the forehead. "Merry Christmas, Hannah. Now and forever."

A word about the author...

Kim Turner writes western historical and contemporary romance. She discovered her passion for writing at a young age with poems, short stories, and journals.

Kim graduated with a Bachelor's of Science in Nursing and holds a Master's Degree in Adult Education. Working as a registered nurse educator/ quality analyst for over thirty years now, she enjoys studying the medical treatments of the old West as well as keeping up with the latest Western movies and television.

While she loves reading anything from highlanders to pirates, she claims to have an unquenchable thirst for the American cowboy. Kim lives south of Atlanta with her husband and calls her greatest accomplishment the birth of one daughter and the adoption of another from China—neither of which came easy.

Kim is a member of RWA and Georgia Romance Writers. Motto: It's All About A Cowboy and the Woman He Loves.